Glimmers of Hope

Kristy Lee

First Published in 2021 by Blossom Spring Publishing
Glimmers of Hope Copyright © 2021 Kristy Lee
ISBN 978-1-8384972-6-2
E: admin@blossomspringpublishing.com
W: www.blossomspringpublishing.com
Published in the United Kingdom. All rights reserved under
International Copyright Law. Contents and/or cover may not be
reproduced in whole or in part
without the express written consent of the publisher.
Names, characters, places and incidents are either products of
the author's imagination or are used fictitiously.

For Joey:
Thank you for being the inspiration behind all the love stories I write.

Thank you to my beta readers. Your input is invaluable!
Rita Potter, Jean Rushing, Jeannie Lakis, and Tara DeWitt.

A special thank you to my niece Molly Hunter for creating the background art used in the cover image.

Most summer nights, the fireflies are her favorite thing, but tonight they haunt her . . . what would normally bring her bliss, torments her instead.

Prologue

The night air is warm, and her breath is erratic as she dips behind the streetlamp attempting to remain unseen. The heels of her Mary Janes tap along the cement as she scurries toward the train station that is the landmark of this small town. It is nine p.m. exactly and she knows the bundle she clutches underneath her favorite thin black cardigan, should only have to wait a few hours before the next train arrives. She hopes that will not be too long as she grips the bundle tightly to provide it comfort while she can.

The clicking of her shoes is the only thing that can be heard this late in such a town, ironically called New Hope. All hope is lost for her but maybe the child still has a chance. The deafening silence is making her even more nervous than she already is. Just a few more steps and she should be at the front door. She ponders if it is the best place to leave the child, but she cannot think of any other choice. She cannot risk the local church, she is there with her mother too often and she fears that, somehow, someone will make the connection back to her. Mostly though she fears the priest figuring it out, figuring out that the baby is the result of the night his nephew, David, took her virginity—pulling her white panties down as she bent over the pew. She had wanted it, wanted him, never really understanding what the consequences of such actions could be. Believing somehow that because he was related to a holy man and was destined to be a priest himself, the sins of the night would be washed away by morning. After several months of no period and a growing belly getting harder to hide, she realized the mistake she had made.

She has not revealed her secret to anyone, even David. She wants to protect him from this because she knows how strict his uncle is and how much trouble David would be in. Maybe by leaving the baby on the steps of the train station, the town will believe that some transient left the child, never connecting it back to her, and never to David.

The lights along the train station are getting bigger and she only has a few more steps to go when a flickering catches her eye. Small lights are running along the side of the train track, and she recognizes them immediately as fireflies. Their flickering seems more intense than usual. She wonders if they are trying to tell her something. Most summer nights, the fireflies are her favorite thing, but tonight they haunt her by flashing their little lights at her like a painful warning, trying desperately to stop her from what she is about to do. What would normally bring her bliss, torments her instead.

Finally making it to the entrance, she glances fervently around, ensuring no soul is in sight before unwrapping her cardigan and pulling out the small, tightly wound child. She pulls the fabric back to check that the life inside is still, in fact, alive. The tiny face has eyes screwed tightly shut, retching her heart so she quickly pushes the fabric back over the girl, not wanting to see the face that will haunt her for the rest of her life. In her desperation to rid the child, she raced from her mother's home without saying a word so she must get back before it is noticed that she is gone. Her mother does not know that she gave birth in the bathtub, stifling her screams into a pillow and cutting the umbilical cord with a dull kitchen knife. She must get back to clean up the mess before her mother sees. Her mother is already asleep but gets up to use the bathroom frequently, so she knows she only has a small window of time to complete this gruesome task.

As a fifteen-year-old good Christian girl, it is

unimaginable that she would get pregnant, and she is desperate to go back to being the person that her mother, and this town, believes her to be. Yet, as she sets the child down on the steps, the lamp overhead casting a dim yellow glow over the blood-stained white towel, she knows she will never be the girl she ought to have been.

Chapter One

Another new school.

Here I go again, walking up the steps of, what is the name again? Oh yea, Lambert High, where I will be forced to meet new students, new teachers, new bullies, new sheep. Starting at a new school in the middle of the last semester of senior year might sound like a nightmare to some, because it is.

Nobody wants to be the "new kid" and I have done it more times than I can keep track of, but I have a system now. I know how to handle this. Walk-in, keep your head down, do not make direct eye contact, find your locker, locate the classroom quickly, sit in the second to last row off to the side—ignore stares—do not draw attention to yourself.

The most critical part of my method: never, under any circumstance, fall in love.

"Being in foster care is hard enough with the moving around, but do yourself a favor and don't date, and definitely don't fall in love. It'll make life so much harder for you when you are forced to leave again. Trust me it is the best thing you can do for yourself," said my heartbroken foster sister when I was just six years old, "love is for fools."

She was older than me and much wiser, so I have taken her words to heart, not wanting to be as miserable as she was in that moment.

My method works. It is full proof. One of the main downsides of the technique, though, is that I have zero friends. I cannot tell you how many foster parents and counselors I have heard say, "Birdie, make friends, it is so important for you to make friends."

This might be easy for them to say but let me tell you it is not easy to do. By the time I start a new school in some new neighborhood, cliques have already been established, social groups already developed. Nobody is looking to add to it either, and not the girl who is too skinny with jet black stringy hair and a bad attitude.

I do not actually have a bad attitude, it's just what I want people to think. It helps keep the bullies and buffoons at bay. Growing up in foster homes does create a tough exterior, though, it is the skin of a survivor.

This is the last semester of high school. In three short months, I will graduate and begin my studies at Alfred University in Alfred, New York. It is my dream liberal arts university tucked away in the western part of the state. I have been working diligently my entire life to make my dream of college come true. Even at a very young age, only ten years old, my parents encouraged me to do well in school so that I may get into college later. After they died, I became determined to see this dream to fruition, for them. Through eleven different foster homes and just as many schools throughout New York and New Jersey, I have managed to maintain a high GPA. Even when I went hungry or was being yelled at by one of the foster parents, I still made it to class every day and did all my homework. My determination and ambition are unmatched, and it is finally happening; I am headed to college on an academic scholarship. My parents left me a college fund in the amount of ten thousand dollars. It might not seem like much to some, but that money will cover the rest of the costs that the scholarship does not. The scholarship covers tuition but there are more costs to attending college that I will need the fund for. Alfred is a private, liberal arts university so it is a bit on the pricier side, but with my parent's help, it can be done.

I should clarify for the purpose of this story that the Wright's were not my biological parents. They raised me from the age of five to age ten. This is the longest I was ever placed in a home and they officially adopted me just three months before their deaths. I loved them and like to think of them as my actual parents. I think they would have wanted that.

Now, as I enter my new high school, I remind myself that I just need to get through the rest of this semester and the summer before it will all come to fruition. That should not be so hard, right?

I cross the crowds of kids desperately seeking my locker—when I make my first blunder of the day: I *trip*.

Papers, pencils, binders, and books go flying, the laminate floor contributing to further my agony as the slick surface spreads the fallen items all over. If you have ever tripped in front of a bunch of mean, hormonal teenagers then you can relate to the horror I am feeling in this moment.

"Dumbass," "Watch out newbie," and "Learn how to walk," are just some of the treasures thrown in my direction.

My method has a wrench in it, but I can still recover, however, I cannot afford another attention-grabbing mistake.

~~~

His name is Austen. I determine he is on the football team, and I suspect he is a complete douche. I make these quick assessments because he is wearing a football letterman jacket and he has a herd of losers surrounding him as he treks towards me. The losers are staring at him and saying his name like it will facilitate a magic wish.

"Austen, are you coming to my house party? It won't be the same without you there."

"Austen, what're you doing for lunch?"

"Austen, you can meet up with us for lunch if you

3

want."

He appears to be the stereotypical hot, rich, popular jock who is probably completely devoid of any real emotion.

Mr. Douche comes across some of my scattered items and is kind enough to kick my binder across the floor with his perfectly polished Gucci tennis shoe just as I was reaching for it, making sure to get plenty of laughs while doing so, hence the douche impression. Have teenage boys not evolved past this type of behavior?

"Play fetch new kid." Ugh. This blending in thing is off to a bad start. I finally gather my stuff, other than a couple of pencils that I sacrifice to the gods of humiliation, and bolt into my class which, luckily, is easy to find.

Biology class, okay I can do this. I find a chair near the back and off to the side and try to collect myself. Just as my embarrassment begins to settle, Mr. Douche walks in.

You. Have. Got. To. Be. Kidding. Me.

Luckily, he sits in the front on the other side of the room and does not seem to notice me.

Thirty minutes later and I have almost forgotten completely about Mr. Douche when I hear, "Why are you staring at me creeper," from across the room. It is Austen and he is looking right at me.

"Yeah, you. I see you staring at me."

"Okay Austen, that's enough, I need you to get back to your reading," says the nerdy teacher wearing glasses too big for his face.

"I will, it's just hard when I'm being stared at. I'm the victim."

I opt to say nothing, I have nothing to say. I have been lost in a daydream and must have been gazing in his direction, but I certainly was not staring at HIM. He is

4

truly horrible. My nemesis. My mortal enemy.

Every eye in the room is on me as now. I wish I had the power of invisibility so that I could fade into the background of this room, disappearing from this place forever.

~~~

High school is a hellish place, I have had loads of bad experiences in high school. That tends to happen when you are always the new kid. I once had a group of mean teenage girls tell me I needed to clean my clothes more because I was attracting flies and then stick gum in my hair. My experience at this school, though, might be the worst yet in large part thanks to the lovely nickname Austen blesses me with: Creeper. This is an impactful nickname for a girl because it is rare. It is memorable. It sticks. My stringy hair and sunken face add to the effect, and by the end of my first day, at whatever school this is, it's clear that the nickname Creeper is here to stay—as I am called it in every class I attend and even have it yelled across the cafeteria to me while I try to eat the chicken nuggets this school is trying to pass off as food. Three-thirty cannot get here soon enough.

By the end of my first day at Lambert High, I have already contemplated numerous plots to end my humiliation including but not limited to: bomb-making, faking my death, and my favorite, going outside and getting hit by a car but, no, I must get through this last semester, so I resign to just take the teasing. Soon it will be all a bad memory. . . at least that is what I keep telling myself.

"Hey Creeper, I know you're obsessed with me but if you don't stop creeping me out, I will have to report it. I shouldn't have to take this kind of abuse." Austen says this as he walks by my locker, sporting a smile as big as the Grand Canyon across his stupid face.

The giggly girls following him are all about the torment as they chime in, "Yeah Creeper, get a life. He would never be into you."

Sudden inspiration from the classic film, *Heathers*, a personal favorite of mine, pops into my head encouraging me to be a little dangerous. I reconsider my previous acceptance of the teasing. There are only two and half months left of high school, I could have some fun with this. I mean it is not like I can get expelled this late in the year, right?

By the way, if you have not seen *Heathers*, I strongly recommend it.

Chapter Two

It is Tuesday morning, a week after the spawning of the Creeper title, and I have perfected a new way to handle my humiliating nickname. By *leaning* into it. Pleasure is found by intentionally staring at Mr. Douche randomly in class and giving him my best, "I will kill you" Creeper face.

To create the perfect Creeper face, one must squint their eyes and part their lips slightly while tucking their chin close to their neck. Let me tell you, it is quite the look. I may even have a lengthy career in modeling.

Austen usually ignores me but yesterday after class he walked by me and said, "You're one scary chick Creeper," and it was the nicest thing anyone had said to me at this school.

After Austen compliments me on my performance, I decide I want to take it up a notch so today, before first period Biology, I take a red marker and scribble Creeper onto my locker, making sure to write the letters in a way I imagine a disturbed serial killer writing them, then use a black marker to draw a smiley face. I tape a small picture of skull that I cut from an anatomy book in the library next to the smile to add to the absurdity.

My creation is a masterpiece. I have recreated it here for your amusement:

I figure that if I scare these imbeciles, they will leave me alone.

I smile all through Biology, reveling in my creation

when I hear my name being called over the intercom.

"Elizabeth Wright please report to the principal's office. Now."

"Ohhhhhh," echo the kids in class as I walk out and down to the office. *Crap,* I hope she does not expel me. I must graduate with high honors in order to meet the requirements of the academic scholarship I have worked so hard for. Suddenly, my artistic masterpiece does not seem so brilliant.

"Ms. Elizabeth, please come in," says the small lady with extremely white teeth.

"I found a few disturbing images and phrases on your locker today. Did you put those there or did someone else?"

"I only put that stuff on there because they are calling me Creeper. I was trying to lean into the taunting. I was just responding to the bullies because they wouldn't leave me alone and stop calling me that," I say as innocently as I can muster.

"Look Elizabeth, you've only been here a couple of weeks, I know a little bit about your situation. I don't want to make it harder on you, I want you to graduate and do well. Your grades are outstanding at every school you attend. Bullying is not tolerated at this school, but neither are references to violence or death, do you understand? I do need you to speak with the school counselor, okay? And take the stuff off your locker."

"Yes. Sorry."

"Head down to see the counselor now, she's expecting you, and there better not be any more disturbing stuff like this coming from you Elizabeth. Consider this your first and final warning."

"Okay."

"What are the names of the kids bullying you, Elizabeth? I will need to have a conversation with them as well."

"That'll only make this worse."

"We have to deal with this, I can't ignore it, I need to know who is bullying you."

"Okay . . . it's Austen."

"Austen Markey?"

"Yes."

"Okay, I'll deal with it, let me know if he bullies you anymore."

"Okay."

"Now get going to the counselor's office."

~~~

Unfortunately, the counselor I am sitting in front of does not share in my sense of humor, "Elizabeth, I am worried about you. Do you think of hurting yourself or others? Are you fascinated with death?"

Oh *geez*.

"No. It was a joke. I thought it was funny. I'm not homicidal or suicidal and, no, I am not fascinated with death. Can I go now? There are just ten weeks of class left and I will be out of here. Just let me get it over with."

"Elizabeth, I think I need to have a conversation with your parents."

"I don't have parents. I live in a foster home and I don't think those people know anything about me. I'm so close to being done with this part of my life, please just let this go for now. I promise I won't cause you any more problems."

"This type of thing is not to be taken lightly."

"This is the least of my concerns."

"You seem very angry Elizabeth, and I'm concerned about that. Can you promise to come to talk to me a few more times before graduation at least?"

Never going to happen lady, "Yeah, sure, but there's nothing *you* can do for me," I say forcefully.

The frightened counselor in a pastel hand-knitted sweater sitting in front of me nods, so I leave the room wondering if maybe I am a Creeper after all.

~~~

As I walk down the hall to my locker to clean off my beautiful artwork, Austen comes out of Biology class. I heard his name over the intercom, but I was already walking down the hall, so I am not able to avoid this encounter.

"Am I being called to the principal's office because of you, Creeper?"

"Um, maybe, I told them you were bullying me."

"Thanks a lot, Creeper, that's just what I need. You better not have gotten me in trouble, or I will make your life a living hell."

"You already have."

"Why are you such a bitch?"

My voice is rising, "I'm the bitch? You are the bitch here, Austen. You kicked my stuff all over after I tripped in the hallway, and you call me Creeper."

"It's not cruel if it's true."

"I'm not a creeper and I wasn't staring at you that day!"

"Fine! Stop yelling, you're going to get us both suspended."

"Whatever, just leave me alone for the rest of the semester."

"With pleasure." Austen saunters off, fists in pockets. I really hate that guy.

Chapter Three

It is the end of the school day as I put my books in my locker and grab my backpack to begin the long walk to the foster home. It takes me about forty-five minutes to get there, but I do not mind. I always walk to any foster home I am living in. I do not take the bus because I do not want to risk the other kids on the bus to see where I am living. It is not because the homes are ever completely filthy or anything, I just do not want anyone to see the other dozen kids staying at the home. It is clear when you walk up to the foster homes I have lived in, that they are places for unwanted children. Children ranging from all ages and races can be seen congregating attempting to survive.

The neighborhood of my latest home is a poor one. The poverty level is apparent thanks to the broken windows that are taped together with duct tape, the rusted bikes propped up against the peeling white paint of the fence that is used to keep the dogs from escaping, the un-mowed lawns, and the overflowing trashcans. There are also a pair of sneakers strung up on the electrical cord hovering over the street. I cannot explain it, but in every poor neighborhood I have lived in, there is always a pair of shoes hanging from the electrical cords.

I am embarrassed. I am ashamed of my situation. I cannot help it. At one time I was almost a normal kid, I had two loving, blue-collar parents who adored me and were raising me in a decent four-bedroom apartment in a middle-class part of the city. This might not sound like much but compared to the conditions I live in now; it was practically the Ritz.

My latest foster parents are nothing like the Wrights. June and Rick West are the type of foster parents who do it for the money and nothing else. They are the type of people who think raising kids is easier than a full-time job. Although "raising" is a bit strong, more like sheltering. June spends the money on electronics and food. It might surprise you just how big my foster mother is, it surprises a lot of people. I am not talking chubby or slightly overweight, I am talking about the type of big where it is hard to stand for longer than two seconds. She sits on the sofa, binge-watching cooking shows all day, every day. The impression of her body is permanently etched into the cushions, buckling under the weight. I have only been living here a few weeks, but I have not seen her leave the house once. I do not know how she does it, I believe I would die of boredom. I mean, how much can you watch on TV? On occasions, she will yell at one of the kids in the home to quiet down or ask one of the older ones to make a fast-food run. She means well, I think. I do not believe her to be mean or evil. She is just locked in her own cage of misery; stuck in a life that she has created but hates.

Her I do not mind, it's the husband that I fear. I have managed to go all this time in the system without being sexually assaulted. This is quite a feat given my circumstances, but I am very careful and trust no one. Rick, who works at a restaurant washing dishes part-time, is interested in me. He stares at me blatantly, running his tongue between the grooves of his missing teeth, the chewing tobacco he has tucked into his cheek staining his tongue a dark brown color. He likes to remind me that I will be eighteen soon and how excited he is for that. Somewhere deep in his mind, I think he believes that by me turning eighteen, I will magically be available to have sex with him. What he does not know is that I plan to move out of this dump the day of my birthday, June third, never to see any of these people again.

Now, to move out of the house on my birthday might

sound simple but it is not. I have nowhere to go and no money. As I walk home, I contemplate a plan for work, having been turned down for several jobs in the last couple of months, when I notice a sign taped to the door outside of the unemployment office.

I stop, and my eye strains to read the faded ink. *Seeking a temporary full time, live-in housekeeper for the summer. Please call to inquire.*

I wonder if they are still hiring because this would be perfect. Money and a place to live? Sounds almost too good to be true. I rip the paper off and stuff it in my pocket, I will call as soon as I get to the home.

~~~

I open the front door and, Felix, the large German shepherd who also happens to be the only decent part of living in this hell hole, runs up to me, wagging his tail. I think he is the only creature living here who notices my comings and goings, other than Rick of course.

"Oh, it's just you. Come back over here Felix," my foster mother barks, a chicken wing sitting on her stomach.

"Can I use your phone for a sec?" It is unusual for a seventeen-year-old girl in these modern times not to have a phone of her own, but I plan to get a cheap one with my first paycheck.

"I guess but don't be on it long, I need it."

I grab the iPhone on the stand next to her, amazed that she would spend so much money on an expensive phone instead of fixing the broken window or having the flickering lights in the hallway looked at, but I digress. I dial the number written on the bottom of the flyer.

A woman answers, "Hello, Maude Whitman speaking."

"Hi, I was calling about your ad for a housekeeper. I am very interested in the position if you're still hiring."

"Yes, we're still hiring. The position is from May to August, and it is live-in. Are you looking for something that temporary and would you be able to reside here during that time?"

"Yes, that would actually work perfectly for me because I need somewhere to work and stay for the summer. I'm headed to college in the fall."

"Wonderful. You're the first person who has said that this arrangement would work. As long as you are eighteen and can clean, you've got the job."

"I will be eighteen on June third."

"Hm, well you won't be able to move in and start working until then."

"Is that okay?"

She pauses, then says, "Yes, we can make that work. What's your name?"

"Elizabeth Wright but I go by Birdie."

"Okay Birdie, do you have any cleaning experience?"

"I have worked at a couple of fast-food places and I did a lot of the cleaning. Things like mopping, cleaning out the fridges and stoves, stuff like that. I don't have a ton of experience but I'm a fast learner and don't mind the work."

"That sounds reasonable. Cleaning is pretty straight forward. We would provide you with a detailed list of what needs to be done each day so it would be fairly self-explanatory. It doesn't pay well, just minimum wage."

"That's fine for me."

"Great, can you stop by for a visit tomorrow afternoon and fill out some forms? I want to see you in person. I also need to run a background check on you. Is that going to be a problem?"

"Not at all. I can be there right after I get done with

class at three-thirty."

"Perfect. The place you will be working is on the North Shore of Long Island, but I have an office I use in Manhattan. Just ring the buzzer and the doorman will let you in. You will need to enter code 303 to get through the gates." She gives me an address to the Manhattan office, and I scribble it on an old receipt.

"Okay, thank you for the opportunity."

~~~

The next day in biology class, Mr. Friedman assigns us partners so that we may have the pleasure of dissecting a frog together. I can't believe they still have kids do this. How is there not an app I can download instead?

Austen has not looked in my direction once since our encounter in the hallway, so I am happy to report that the torment is over.

I am usually relieved when a teacher picks our partners instead of letting us choose our own because this prevents the unavoidable social embarrassment of nobody wanting to pair up with me and then I am left with the smelly kid that is even more of a social pariah than myself. Today, however, my nightmares come true as Mr. Friedman assigns me to work with the worst person humanly possible.

"Elizabeth, you're with Austen."

"It's Birdie," annoyance apparent.

"Fine, Birdie, you're with Austen."

Austen? Are you kidding me? Of all people.

Austen rolls his eyes and saunters over to my table, dropping his books down and sighing, "Don't worry I won't talk to you and you get to do all of the work."

"Wonderful."

Mr. Friedman lays a dead frog on everybody's table

and I get to dissecting. Poor froggy. He gave his life so that a bunch of gross high school students could cut him open while gagging.

"You do have to participate if you want the grade Mr. Markey," Mr. Friedman says to Austen as he weaves between groups.

Austen sighs and puts his phone down, picks up a pencil and the assignment. "Okay, we are supposed to label and find each of these organs. You find 'em, and I'll write 'em."

I nod but do not say anything. I just want this to end.

I finish the horrid task and identify the organs all while Austen finishes writing the information on the assignment. He is sitting close to me so I can get a good look at him. I have no idea why everyone is so obsessed with him. I guess he is attractive, I mean if you are into basic stereotypical rich white dudes with no personalities. His brown hair is messy, and he wears his t-shirts a bit too tight. I think he is going for James Dean, but he is failing miserably. A skinny silver chain is around his neck, the end of the necklace is tucked under his shirt collar and I wonder if it is a cross. That would be hilarious if the king of douche dared to wear a cross given how much of an ass he is.

"Really? Staring at me again? What's your problem?"

"Oh, get over yourself. I'm just trying to figure out why everyone is so obsessed with you. You seem pretty basic to me."

"If I'm so basic, why do you stare at me all the time?"

"Because you call me Creeper. So, I creep. It's funny."

"You are one weird chick, you know that?"

"That's what people keep telling me."

"Why'd you put that stuff on your locker, you seem like you are really disturbed or something."

I shrug, trying my best to convey nonchalance.

"Maybe I am."

Austen looks up from his phone and makes eye contact, an odd feeling settles in my stomach as he does, "Look, if you want some advice, try to wear a lot of makeup and change your hair and clothes. If you work it, hard, you might pass for average. It would help you to make friends, you know, if you weren't so gross to look at."

Damn, *Gross*? I knew I was weird but gross? Gross is the smelly kid that sits in the corner and talks to himself. Gross is the kid who is too stupid to know to wear deodorant and shower. Gross is not me. I do not stink. Or do I? I tilt my head toward my chest, sniffing my shirt slightly. My clothes are old and hand-me-downs I got from other foster kids. I have a few shirts I picked up for a dollar or two at the thrift store, but I do clean them so they should not smell. Now, more than ever, I wish I had something new to wear for once.

I try to look unaffected by the gross comment, but my pride has taken a hit, hiding in a corner of my heart like a wounded dog.

After he drops this amazing knowledge, Austen opens his binder and much to my horror, I see a brochure sticking out the inside pocket.

Surely, I am seeing things, this must be a bad dream that I just have not woken up from yet.

Alfred University is written across the top of the brochure.

Why does he have that?

"Alfred University? Tell me you're not going there."

"Yeah, I have to. It is my mother's alma mater and she's forcing me to. What's it to you Creeper? Gonna stalk me or somethin'?"

I roll my eyes, "I'm just surprised that you're going to college, you seem pretty dumb."

Austen appears slightly wounded by my comment and for a split second, I feel bad but brush it away quickly. He deserves it.

I do not want him to know that I am going to the same school as him. Alfred University is a big enough place that I should be able to get by without seeing him there at all. Or if I do, it will just be in passing so I should not have to worry about it.

I have worked so hard to get into college, I am not going to let some high school moron ruin it for me. Besides, I am sure it will be a short-lived concern of mine as he looks like the type who will drop out because he parties too much.

Chapter Four

My dreams of attending college have gotten me through the hardest moments of my life. Just knowing that there is something better coming over the horizon has saved me from falling into a pit of despair more times than I can count. I miss my adoptive family so much sometimes it physically hurts, sending a sharp pain into the base of my neck. When I get too sad thinking of them, I remember the dream they had for me and it lifts me up. I lost the Wrights to a simple thing. A car accident. They were headed home from date night, I was waiting for them with the babysitter and the two other foster kids who were even younger than me, when they switched lanes without looking, hitting a van, and losing control of the vehicle.

They died instantly. Or at least that is what the cops said but I often wonder if they just say that to try to make people feel better. Not only was I with them the longest but I liked them the most out of all my foster parents. They were just good people, and, unlike all the others, they wanted *me* and adopted me as their own. They were always so nice to me too. They never yelled but would handle every situation with love and a smile. I did not even know people like that existed. They loved me and I know that. They were a couple in their forties who weren't able to have children of their own, so they opened their home to four foster kids. Emily, who was older than me and gave me the sage advice to avoid love at all cost, had to leave because her birth mother wanted custody again, even though Emily did not want to leave the Wrights. She loved them, too. Then there were two who are younger than me, an infant named Mary and a one-year-old boy they adopted from China named Li Wei. I often wonder what happened to them. We were all split up among separate foster homes. I heard a few years later that Mary was adopted. I hope she is doing okay. They were the closest thing I ever had to a real family. I do not have many memories of my parents, but the ones I do have, I hold on to tightly.

One memory that sticks with me more than most is the memory of my adoptive mom, Carol Wright, reading to me from her favorite book, *Pride and Prejudice.* I was way too young to understand it, but I enjoyed watching her face light as she read.

"Read this when you are a teenager, then re-read it as an adult, and keep reading it throughout your life. It'll keep surprising you, revealing new details to you each time you open it. It'll teach you lessons throughout your life. Trust me, love," she told me this as we snuggled together in my pink themed bedroom while I clutched the doll that she gave to me the first day they brought me home.

I still have the doll, Ariel from the Little Mermaid, and her copy of *Pride and Prejudice*, but that is all. I do not even have a picture of them. I remember Carol's long blond hair pulled back into a ponytail, her lavender scent filling my nose as she spoke. I remember my adoptive father Frank, his balding hairline and kind smile. The memories of them are the best I have. They represent the only time in my life I have ever known true happiness, they were the closest I ever came to normal. Now, every year on my mother Carol's birthday, July tenth, I re-read *Pride and Prejudice* while clutching that small doll.

It is because of them that I came across Alfred University in the first place. It is a vivid memory I have of them, when we went on a road trip to get out of the city, just the three of us to celebrate my birthday. I remember they used to do that, allow each kid to pick what they wanted to do for their birthday, and I wanted to go on a road trip just with them. I did not want to share the attention with my foster siblings. We drove through a small town we had never heard of, Alfred, and saw a university.

My adoptive father, Frank, looked at me in the rearview mirror, his blue eyes shining, and said, "This place is incredible, Birdie. If you work hard and get good grades, you could go here one day. We have already started a college fund for you and your siblings."

He always called me Birdie. He would say, "Fly my little Birdie, fly," as he twirled me around and around while I laughed, feeling more like a bird than a bird ever could. I have held on to the nickname in honor of him.

That road trip was the last memory I have of my parents, they would pass just a few weeks later. I became obsessed with *Pride and Prejudice* and the idea of attending this beautiful university tucked away in the hills of New York.

You see, when a person experiences happiness but loses it, they tighten their grip on the memories from when they were happy out of fear that they will lose them too, leaving them with nothing.

~~~

You might be curious as to what landed me in foster care to begin with. Well, let me tell you it is quite the story. You know how you hear in the news about babies being left at churches, stoops, and fire stations but you never actually meet anyone who was left as a child at a church, stoop, or fire station? Now you can say you have. Me. I am one of those rare people who got abandoned as a newborn, never to be claimed. It is a strange story and I learned at a young age that it is so much easier to just tell people my parents were the Wrights and they died in a tragic accident. In a lot of ways, I wish it were the truth as it is easier to explain than "I don't know who my parents were, I was abandoned out front of a train station in some random small town in Pennsylvania." Just imagine the number of questions you would get from a story like that.

I did receive a clue as to who my biological parents might have been in the form of a letter from the adoption agency that I received three years ago when I was sixteen and at the height of puberty and uncertainty. I only read the letter once, before folding it up and hiding it away between the last page and back cover of *Pride and Prejudice*. I have not looked at it since. The details of the letter I cannot recall but the gist of it was that a man who lived in New Hope, Pennsylvania, was interested in contacting me and obtaining a DNA test. He suspected he might be my birth father. When I received this letter at the delicate age of sixteen, I did not know what to think about it. I tucked it away in a dark corner of my mind, ignoring it until a time came when I could handle such information.

Now and again, I am tempted to read the letter, but fear grips me and pushes me away as though the letter has some kind of forcefield around it. I am not sure I want to know the story of how I came to be abandoned. I was not wanted, so in the end what difference does it make who put me there? Really though, I am just afraid to know the truth.

~~~

The last weeks at Lambert High fly by, my encounters with Austen and being called Creeper fade into the background as everyone's attention is focused on graduating, which allows insulting me to take a back seat.

In fact, that day in Biology is the last day Austen speaks to or looks at me again, which is delightful.

Before I know it, I am standing in a black graduation gown in line to collect my diploma. Looking at the kids around me and the crowds in the stands, all waving, I am too embarrassed to be the only one not, so, I wave pretending like I have someone to wave to. It sounds pathetic, I know, but it is oddly therapeutic. Instead of waving to a person, I wave goodbye to this life; my life as a foster kid; my life as a troubled youth; my life as the kid without a family.

I take a deep breath and exhale, "Goodbye."

Chapter Five

The last few weeks spent at the foster home before I turn the magic number of eighteen are mostly uneventful. I spend my days counting down the hours until my birthday. I have an actual countdown on a chalkboard behind my pillow, and I try to stay out of the way and remain mostly invisible. I hang out at the small park that is only a short thirty-minute walk away and I sit under an old oak tree reading to kill time. I only return to the home after ten p.m. when I know Rick has left for the late shift at the restaurant and my foster mother has fallen asleep on the couch. I have not mentioned to anyone that I am moving out on my birthday or where I am going or what I will be doing with my summer but I have only lived in this house for less than four months so I am pretty sure that my presence will not be missed. A couple of the kids might miss me though. I share a room with two other foster kids, little kids under the age of five, who have come to count on me being there to get them up in the morning for breakfast. They look just as lost as I feel. I wish I could help them more, but it is time for me to go.

I want nothing more than freedom. Foster care has been my prison, tying me to people I do not wish to be tied to. It is not the kids that I mind, it is never the kids. It is the adults. Adults are the ones that you cannot trust. I have the desire to one day become a foster parent so that I can be the type of parent that I always needed but rarely got.

The Wrights were the only people who ever really wanted me. They fell in love with me and I with them. We were a family. At the other homes I have been placed in, I always got the impression that I was not what they wanted. I was either too quiet, too weird, or too old. That is one of the things they never tell you, it is usually only infants who get adopted. Once you pass that cute baby stage, nobody wants you. It is a hard reality, but it is reality.

The Wrights were my only exception.

~~~~

Ever since the Wrights died, my birthday is not something that I ever make a big deal of. I usually do not tell anyone about it and just spend the day holding my breath waiting for it to pass like all the other days.

This birthday is different, though, because I have a real reason to celebrate. I am finally eighteen and free from the clutches of the foster care system. Today, I am an adult who is about to embark on the rest of her life. Nobody can tell me where to live or where to go to school or what to do anymore.

It is one a.m. I am already packed and sitting at a bus station, not bothering to say goodbye to anyone in the house except for Felix, who wagged his tail and licked my face as I whispered to him, "I love you, Felix, be a good boy." I will miss that mutt. I kissed the foreheads of the two little kids I share a room with while they slept and left them both a note telling them that everything will be okay, it will get better.

Sitting on this bus bench with my trash bag of belongings, I look up to the sky, clouds hanging overhead skewing my view of any stars.

"Happy birthday to me," I say to myself out loud.

"Happy birthday," says the homeless guy trying to sleep on the steps of the building behind me.

"Thanks, man."

~~~~

It takes several hours before I arrive at the house that I will call home for the summer. It is the break of dawn as I am greeted by a man who unlocks the metal gate for me, asking me to follow him. His name is Edwardo and he's the doorman. He is super skinny and looks like he thinks smiling is a sin. I follow, walking up a stone path, leading to the house, if you can call it that. I have never seen anything quite like it, reminding me of some grand European castle. The North Shore is an area known for excessive wealth and I can see why as each home is more elaborate than the last. I had to take two busses, a ferry, and taxi to get here, using the last of my small savings.

The stone exterior compliments the stone path perfectly; stained glass windows reflect the light of the sun, casting colorful shadows over the perfectly manicured garden; creating an almost churchlike impression. Edwardo leads me inside, through open large wooden doors into a waiting area with staircases on each side. Porcelain statues are at the bases of the staircases, statues of fat babies and beautiful women. In the middle of the entryway is a rug made of real tiger fur, even the tiger's head is still attached to the rug. Man, rich people are so weird.

I expect to meet the lady who hired me, and I am right as I see her walking down the stairs towards me.

"Hello, Elizabeth, nice to see you again. I can't remember all of what I told you when we met so forgive me if I repeat myself, I manage the grounds here as well as several other properties. Come with me, I will be showing you to your room." Maude motions me to follow her as she continues her speech, "you'll be provided a list of chores that the Markey's will expect you to complete each day. The Markey's want me to emphasize to you that they are not your caretakers. They expect you to take care of yourself so if you are hungry, go to the kitchen, if you need to go somewhere, call a cab, if you need something, go get it. They're simply providing you with the room at no cost and an hourly wage of the minimum. Understand?"

"Yes, absolutely no problem."

"Please don't touch their things other than when you are cleaning them and be extra careful with their statues and paintings. They are priceless."

"I understand."

Maude leads me to a dungeony part of the house, the dark lower level, where I assume I will be staying.

"Oh, this will be perfect for me to practice my witchcraft." Maude looks back at me with an unimpressed expression. "Sorry, I was just kidding."

"Hmm," she murmurs this as she arches one eyebrow. *Yikes,* tough crowd.

The room I am provided with has one small window high on the wall, a bed, closet, and television.

"It's rather dreary in here but this is where they want you to stay. Is this going to be a problem?"

"No, not at all." What is considered dreary to her is dreamy to me.

"And please Elizabeth, no witchcraft on the grounds." Wow, I do not think this lady has ever heard a joke in her life.

"No problem Maude, I will keep my crystals and broomstick in the closet."

"Hmm."

~~~

Liza and Aiesha are too cool for words. They work on the grounds of the, what I am referring to now as, the castle. Liza does the gardening and Aiesha takes care of the horses. They are on the welcoming committee at my door within moments of Maude leaving me to unpack.

"Is that all you have? Do you need help bringing anything else up? How did you get here? Where are you from?"

"Um, this is all I have, and I took a couple of buses, a ferry, and a cab to get here," I say trying not to show how nervous I am. I hope they like me.

"Oh, wow! My name is Aiesha, and this is Liza."

Aiesha's smile is genuine, and I think to myself how rare it is that I get to see a genuine smile. Liza does not smile at me, her perfectly styled blond hair and heavy makeup reminding me of the types of girls you see on social media.

"It's nice to meet you both, I'm Birdie. I'm the new housekeeper but will only be here until August."

Liza reaches out her hand to shake mine, her loose tank top and low-rise jeans giving off a sexy vibe.

"Hi, Birdie. We know all about you already. The regular housekeeper is out because she just had a baby but will be back after a few months. If you want to know the gossip, it's Master Heath's love child."

"Master Heath?"

"Yes, Lady Mary Markey's husband. Well, technically, but he doesn't much act like one. I mean, we have all slept with him at some point. They are the owners of this place. Neither of them are here a lot, they both travel for work."

"You've both slept with Heath Markey?" Markey? Isn't that Austen's last name?

"I haven't and would never," says Aiesha, the stud in her nose sparkling.

"Okay fine, not everyone. Not Aiesha and I don't think Edwardo has." The women giggle and cannot tell if they are being serious or not.

"Do you both live here as well?"

"No, we share an apartment in the city. We just come here three days a week. We made a special trip though to meet you, well that and to hang out by the pool. Maude doesn't mind if we use the pool as long as it's not on a workday and the Wright's aren't home. We will be out back if you want to join."

"Thank you, I don't swim and am kinda tired so I'm going to sleep for a bit. Isn't it a bit early in the day to go swimming?"

"No, it's just warm enough, plus we like to get out there when no one else is using it."

"Who else uses it?"

"The Markey's prized possession, their son. He lives here during the summers and is by the pool every day by noon with his moron friends. Liza and I like to chill without being forced to talk to a bunch of high school jocks."

"They are not high school jocks anymore, they just graduated."

"Whatever, I will always see them as jocks. Stay away from them Birdie, they're not worth your time," Aiesha says, warning me.

"Okay, I will. See you both later then?"

"Sure, will give you a tour of the grounds. The Markey's own a lot of property and it's gorgeous. We will share all of its secrets with you."

"Thanks, Aiesha, that sounds wonderful."

"Later, Birdie," Aiesha says as she turns to leave, her dreadlocks swinging as she does, revealing a tattoo of a rose on the back of her neck.

I circle back to the high school jock son comment. What are the odds that it's Austen? It can't be, right?

Chapter Six

It is now ten in the morning when a loud thud jolts me awake. It sounds like it is coming from a room next to mine.

Thud.

Must be another person moving in as I can hear the sliding of bags and the rolling of suitcases.

Then I hear him.

"Okay mom, I put your precious shit in the scary dungeon . . . No, they won't get damaged. Nobody comes down here anyway except for the help . . . Why couldn't Edwardo bring this stuff down here? Yes, I know he hurt his back, but I am not here to do chores."

I rub the sleep out of my eyes, his voice . . . it sounds oddly familiar . . . reminding me of someone, but who?

Oh no. NO.

IT CAN'T BE HIM.

I slide out of my bed, pull on the robe I stole from a couple of foster homes ago, and tiptoe to the door, quietly opening it. I will just casually walk by the room and look inside. Totally a normal thing to do.

I walk out, scooting on my socks to not make a sound, and quickly sprint by the room next to me, only glancing in for a second.

Shit.

AUSTEN.

"Creeper? Is that you?"

I slide back around, standing in front of his door.

"Why the hell are you in my house?"

"Um, I work here."

"Are you kidding me? Why? Did you do this on purpose?"

"NO! I did not know you lived here! I had no idea! I wouldn't want to be in the same house as you for

30

anything—you slimy meathead!"

"Ok, damn, calm down. I just wasn't expecting to see you creeping in my house. I was hoping to never see you again after graduation. You live here, too?"

"Yes, in the room next door. I am the temp housekeeper while the other is away with her new baby."

"Man, what are the odds that you would be working at my house this summer. I must have some bad karma or something."

"You do and it's because you're an ass."

"Whatever Creeper, you always get so worked up. Just stay out of my hair, okay? It shouldn't be a problem since I never see the help anyway."

"Fine, I'll stay away from you but only if you don't call me Creeper anymore. Otherwise, I'm going to make your life a living hell."

"Are you threatening me? Because I can fire you in a second."

Crap.

"No, I am not threatening you. Please I need this job, can we just stay away from each other for a few months?"

"That's more like it. Hope to not see you around, Creeper."

Ugh. He is truly the worst. This might not be as great as I originally thought.

~~~

I just need to survive for three months and then I will be in Alfred. Surviving in a castle is not the difficult part, avoiding Austen is. I have only been here for two weeks and I keep running into him by accident but, of course, he always thinks it is intentional.

"The surprise run-ins need to stop, Creeper," Austen

says as he puts surprise in air quotes.

"I'm not doing this on purpose. I'm just trying to do my job, Austen. And please, call me Birdie."

"HA! Is that your name? And you think that is better than Creeper?"

Heat is rising in my cheeks, inflaming my skin.

"Yeah well, it's what I go by. My real name is Elizabeth. Now move, I need to get back to vacuuming."

"You know, I've never vacuumed in my life."

"Yeah, I believe that."

Austen feigns offense as he trots away down one of the many marble staircases. He is unpleasant but it is made worse when he has his friends with him. All they do is talk about sex and drink vodka and lay around the pool. When his macho friends are over, I hide in my room, heeding Aiesha's advice. I cannot run into them; the ridicule is too much to risk.

One of the chores on my to-do list today is to wipe down the pool furniture and it is the last thing on my list, so I put away the vacuum and go outside. It is already four p.m. so Austen's friends should be gone, they usually leave around two. I should have checked first, though, because I am already outside when I notice two of Austen's dumbass friends sitting by the pool and Austen pulling his shirt off so that he can dive in.

Crap. I quickly retreat behind the landscaping, hoping to remain unseen. I will just have to clean the furniture later tonight after his friends are gone. Now to figure out how to get back in the house without being noticed. I sprint back to the backdoor and slip in as quietly as possible, holding my breath as though it will make me invisible. Once inside the door I slide down to the floor and sit for a moment, catching my breath. The door does not shut completely, and I can hear Austen and his friends talking.

"Hey, was that Creeper? From high school? I swear that was that same chick you used to tease. Why she here? Are you hooking up with her dude?"

"No, I'm not hooking up with her. She works here."

"She works here? Doing what?"

"She's the housekeeper for the summer."

"Dude, that's so freaking weird that Creeper is your housekeeper. How did we not know about this?"

"Didn't see why it mattered."

"We should pull a prank on her."

"Yeah, man. Let's pour fake blood on the floor or in a mop bucket or something. She's into that dark shit. Remember that skull thing on her locker? I think she has real problems man. You should be careful having her here. She might be plotting to kill you or something man."

"No, she isn't. We're not going to prank her. Just drop it."

I stand up to flee back to the safe space of my room. I am surprised Austen didn't use this opportunity to tear me apart to his friends. What is that about? Maybe he is not quite as horrendous as he lets on.

~~~

It is now midnight and I have finished cleaning the pool furniture. Although, I will just have to clean it next week again. I can see why they need a live-in housekeeper; the cleaning never ends. That is the problem with having a house this big. I put the cleaning products back into the storage closet, the one that is tucked away under one of the staircases in the back of the house. Apparently rich people never like to see any sign of cleaning supplies, I guess they want to give the illusion that their house is too expensive to get dirty. Before going back to my room, I need to eat, so I slip into the kitchen quietly, flipping the light switch on and opening one of the three huge refrigerators. I seek refuge in the form of a sandwich. I take the ham and cheese out and begin to assemble it on the granite countertop when the unthinkable happens.

Austen walks in.

And he is shirtless.

My God.

There are many problems with this scenario because, one, I do not want to see Austen at midnight, two, I damn well do not want to see him without a shirt on, and three, it is made so much worse by the fact that his body is basically perfect.

"Really Creeper? Why're you in my kitchen?"

"To eat, obviously."

"You eat our food, too? Wow, we give you everything."

"YOU don't give me anything. This is your parents' food, not yours."

"Technicalities."

Austen hops up on the counter beside me, grabs my sandwich, and takes a bite out of it like the animal that he is.

"I was going to eat that."

"So."

There is no use fighting with the spawn of Satan, so I get another slice of meat and cheese to make another.

"Why're you working here?" Austen says this with his mouth full.

"Because I need the money and somewhere to live before college."

"YOU are going to college?"

"Yes, on academic scholarship," I say remembering the Alfred University brochure in his binder, hoping it does not come up. I need to change the subject, and fast.

"I heard you with your friends by the pool."

"So?"

"They suggested pulling a prank on me and I heard you say no. Why? I would've thought that if anyone wanted to be mean to me, it'd be you."

"I think you have the wrong impression of me."

"I doubt that."

"Look, I know I was kind of a jerk in the beginning,"

"Kind of?"

"Okay, fine. But I'm a pretty decent guy."

"I'll believe that when I see it," I say rolling my eyes.

"Why are you so angry all the time?"

"I'm not angry all the time. I think you have the wrong impression of me."

"You screamed at me in the hallway."

"You called me a bitch."

"Okay, whatever, so maybe we both have the wrong impression of each other."

I consider this, "Maybe you're right, Austen."

Austen takes another big bite of my sandwich, "Why don't you just live with your parents until school starts?"

"They're dead."

"Geez, Birdie, I'm sorry."

"Did you, Austen Markey, just offer a shred of human decency?"

"See, I'm not so bad. Most people think I'm great," Austen says as he smiles a big smile, revealing the food in his mouth.

"Yeah, not really. They just think your money is great."

"I have feelings ya know."

"So do I."

"Touché, Birdie, touché."

Austen finishes my sandwich and slides back off the

counter. I try not to stare at his chest, but it is not easy. It is annoying that someone so shitty can look so good.

"Later Birdie, thanks for the sandwich."

"Sure thing, jerk," Austen turns back at me and smiles. Apparently, he enjoys being called a jerk.

Chapter Seven

Liza and Aiesha let me join them for lunch on the days they are working. They like to make sandwiches and congregate under an old tree near the horse barn. Liza usually talks about the garden and boys while Aiesha talks about Jasper and Kevin. It took me a while to realize that when she mentioned Jasper and Kevin that she was not talking about people, but horses.

It is noon on the dot as I make my way down the stone path towards the old oak tree. I can see Liza and Aiesha already sitting out there, drinking iced tea in the shade of the leaves.

"Hey girl!"

"Hey! I brought some sodas in case you wanted something other than tea." I hand them the cans as I cross my legs and sit beside them.

"Thanks. We're glad you're here. We need you to help settle an argument."

"Oh no, what is it?"

"Liza thinks it is perfectly okay to sleep with a married man and I think it's wrong. What do you think Birdie?"

"I agree with you Aiesha, it's wrong."

"I just don't see how it's wrong for me. He's the married one, not me."

I offer my view, "But you're contributing to the decision. Why are you even asking, Liza? You're gorgeous, you could have anyone."

"Exactly, and I want Heath."

"Gross, girl. You hooked up with him once already, isn't that enough? Plus, he got the last housekeeper pregnant, you don't find that disturbing?" Aiesha's eyebrows are raised in disgust.

"Don't be so judgmental, I like him, he's hot."

"But he is, one, your boss, two, way old, and three, married."

"That's what makes it more fun."

I cannot say I understand Liza but she seems way more experienced than me and I am so desperate for her to like me that I choose to agree with her, "I won't judge you, Liza. It's ultimately his decision to cheat or not."

"Yes, I win, you owe me ten bucks, Aiesha."

~~~

It is another sunny summer afternoon at the castle. The large windows in the main room are open, allowing a warm breeze throughout. With the windows open, I can hear the bugs whistling. It is a perfect summer day and I wish I could enjoy it outside.

The sun is high as I mop the hallway at the top of the stairs, light is shining in onto the wet black and white checkered floor. I can hear giggling and I recognize it to be Liza. I go to the window and glance down to the pool. Liza is walking away from Austen who is floating on a pizza-shaped floaty. He does that a lot; rich kids never seem to have much to do.

He is left out there all alone, the heat glistening off his chest, the sun reflecting in his sunglasses. The desire to go down there and dip my toes in the cool water is so strong, I can no longer resist. I have never stepped foot in the pool here. I do not want to risk getting fired, but he is all alone so I should be safe. I do not think Austen would fire me for putting my toes in the water. Plus, I am pretty sure only his parents or Maude can fire me, and both are nowhere to be seen.

I prop the mop against the railing and slip down the stairs. The sun slaps my face as I open the backdoor, reminding me how unprepared I am for a dip in the pool.

I saunter over, trying desperately to look cool as I approach the water.

Austen notices me right away, "What're you doing, Creeper? You clean the pool, too?"

I hate this guy.

"No, I just want to feel the cool water. Is that a crime? You going to have me fired over it?" I am standing over his stupid pizza-shaped floaty now, my hands on my hips, blocking his sun.

"No, geez, you're so sensitive. I was just teasing you."

"Whatever," I say this as I pull off my beat-up tennis shoes and peel away my holey socks. I sit on the edge of the pool and dip my big toe, ever so gently, into the water.

"It won't bite."

"I haven't been in a pool since I was nine years old so leave me alone. Let me enjoy this moment, Austen."

I gather bravery and dip my entire right foot into the cool water, pleasure being the only word that comes to mind. The contradiction of the heat of the sun next to the cool water is magic.

"I've never seen anyone enjoy putting their foot into a pool more than you. You're so weird."

"You're just incapable of enjoying the simple pleasures, cretins never know true joy."

"I don't know what a cretin is, but I assume it's an insult. I know joy."

"No, you don't. You have pleasures all around you, at your fingertips, but you're jaded to them. You expect them. You don't derive pleasure from them. I see you daily, Austen, and I have never seen you really notice any of the stuff around you."

Austen contemplates this before responding, "You're probably right."

"You should stop and take a moment to appreciate the

things around you. I mean you live in a castle filled with beauty."

"How do I do that?"

"Slow down, stop, and admire. Take in all the information your senses are telling you."

"Hm . . . I might try that."

Is Austen Markey taking my advice? Strange, but I am too distracted by the sensation of cold water on my warm skin to care. If this is how the other half live, sign me up.

Chapter Eight

This party is popping. I realize that cool people do not say 'this party is popping' but it is the best way I can describe what is going on around me. This also happens to be the first party I have ever been to, and I have no idea how to act.

Aiesha and Liza are wearing matching Nirvana t-shirts, swaying to some band I have never heard of, looking as young and glamorous as humanly possible. Their ease and simplicity at life are contagious so party-goers swarm them, just wanting to somehow be a part of it, a part of them.

I stand back and admire, drinking a stale beer out of a red solo cup, leaning against the wall, melding into the wallpaper.

Every corner of this house party has a person either standing, sitting, or laying in it. I am not sure who owns this house, but I almost feel bad for them, noticing the spilled beer soaking into the wooden floors.

I wish I were cool enough to be here. The truth is, I am lucky to be here at all. I am an extra invited by my cool acquaintances who asked me to come out of the kindness of their hearts. I take it all in, the people, the dancing, the drinking, the fun, the carefree feeling. I wish I belonged here and was a part of this experience instead of being the observer, the fly on the wall.

Freddy, an overly confident musician with a skinny mustache that on most would be disgusting, but is somehow adorable on him, shouts, "Hey, everyone! Let's play seven minutes in heaven! Gather around!"

A herd of drunken sheep flock to Freddy's side, including a stumbling Austen who I pretend not to notice. Why is he at the same party that Liza and Aiesha invited me to? I would never have guessed them to hang with the same crowd. I stay in my spot, leaned against the wall, trying desperately to appear cool and mysterious.

"Hey, you over there! Hot mysterious chick!"

Freddy is looking right at me. Does he think I am hot? AND mysterious? YES, I cannot believe this is happening, I am being noticed and not as the weird or strange girl but as HOT and MYSTERIOUS. WOW. Maybe I am not just a fly on the wall after all.

"What?" I say pretending to be uninterested as I attempt to put my perceived coolness on full display.

"I dare you to play seven minutes in heaven with this guy," his hand lands on Austen's shoulder.

"Um, I don't think so."

"BOO, boooo!" Everyone is joining in, really?

"Come on, don't be lame! Do it! What are you afraid of? Do you like him or something?"

"She definitely does. She has been my stalker since high school."

"Oh, get over yourself Austen, you're the last person I would ever be into."

"What's the problem? If you don't like him, it's just kissing. It doesn't mean anything."

Every person in the room is staring at me now.

This is my nightmare.

"I don't care. What about you, Austen? Afraid you'll fall in love with me or something?"

Never one to turn down a challenge, Austen pushes through the crowd and stands in front of me and says, "Let's go."

"Ohhhhh," the sheep bellow.

I reluctantly follow Austen upstairs to a small closet as the sheep follow us.

He motions me inside and pulls the door shut behind him, the hordes of people crowd outside, "Okay, seven minutes starts now! I better see some lipstick on your

42

face when you come out, Austen!"

"So, what are we just going to sit in here for seven minutes?" I ask, sitting on a shoebox, the dim light above illuminating the floor just enough that I know I do not want to sit directly on it.

"This place is disgusting."

"It's just a party house."

"What it must be like to have extra houses at your disposal for such activities."

"Yup, I'm jealous," Austen says as he plops right on the floor next to me, not concerned about the filth.

"Why? You're probably richer than all of these people."

"Yeah, but my parents won't give me a party house."

"Oh, you poor bastard."

Austen rolls his eyes and says, "What're you even doing here anyway? Did Aiesha and Liza invite you or something?" Austin looks down at a stain on his sky-blue t-shirt, "Crap, not my new shirt." I wish I had a new shirt to worry about.

"Yes, they're my friends. Or at least I hope they are. Why're you here? You friends with them, too?"

"If by friends, you mean women I'm having sex with, then yes."

I respond with an exaggerated eye roll, "You're not having sex with both of them. There is no freaking way."

"No, but I'm sleeping with Liza." Oh my god, is Liza having sex with Austen AND his dad? Does Austen know this? I'm too afraid of the answer to ask.

"Wow, she's so beautiful, though. I'm surprised she'd be into you."

"Harsh, what do you think is so wrong with me? Most people think I'm a catch."

"They must be idiots."

"Look, those guys are going to be all over me if we

don't make out. Why don't we just do it for a couple of seconds so I can get some of your makeup on me and call it good?"

"I am not wearing makeup, just some lip-gloss."

"That'll work, it should be noticeable since I don't wear lip-gloss."

"This is horrifying. The stuff of nightmares."

"It is just kissing, Birdie. It's not a big deal. You have kissed before, right?"

The peck on the cheek from the little neighbor boy when I was nine drifts into my head, but I am sure that is not the type of kissing Austen is referring to.

"Of course, don't be ridiculous."

"Okay, so let's just get it over with."

Am I going to do this? Have my first make-out session with my mortal enemy? What a terrible memory. I can't tell him that I have never kissed anyone before, he would tease me relentlessly, and I cannot leave this closet because then everyone will think I am lame. I guess this is happening.

Austen leans his head down towards mine and I brace myself for impact. I expect the worst, grossest possible experience, but when his lips touch mine, I'm surprised.

His lips are soft, his kiss gentle. I anticipated this brute to kiss like one but instead, it is the opposite. After a beat, Austen dips his tongue into my mouth and I suddenly become very aware of my breath and quickly break contact.

"I've been drinking stale beer."

Austen looks at me with surprise, "So have I."

He puts his hand on the back of my neck and pulls me back into him, kissing me until I begin to feel my body melt with warmth spreading to the tips of my toes.

Damn this is nice. Too nice.

I pull away, "Is that good enough?"

"Sure Birdie, you don't have to be so weird about it."

I am panicked, I know that was not nearly as good for him as it was for me. I am sure he has had many kisses, and most were better.

"I'm not being weird; I just don't like kissing you is all."

"Whatevs, it's been about seven minutes. I'm out of here." Austen stands up and storms out.

The drunken herd is not outside the door like they promised, the short attention span striking down their ability to care about anything for longer than five seconds.

~~~

Aiesha pays for a cab for me to get back to the castle. Once in my cave, I tuck myself into my covers and try in vain not to think about that kiss. It lingers in my head and on my lips though, betraying me.

Several hours of not being able to sleep later, a bang on my door startles me.

Austen.

I hop out of bed and creak open my door to chastise him, "Austen, what're you doing? It's three a.m., just go to bed."

"Birdie, Birdie, Birdie. If I could, I would."

"What do you mean?"

"No keys."

Austen's swaying is so bad, I think he might fall over.

"You don't need keys, you're already inside. Just go up to your bed."

"Can't."

"Well, guess you are sleeping in the hall then."

"Don't act mean. You won't let me sleep out here."

"You can't sleep in here!"

"Why? I won't touch you," Austen pushes the door open and I fall back.

"What're you doing? This is my room and my bed is not big enough for both of us."

"Shhhhhh."

Austen is on his back on top of my bed, shuffling around drunkenly.

Crap. Now what?

"Okay, Austen you can stay here but don't touch me. I'm going to lay next to you only because I have nowhere else to lay."

"Why do you hate me so much?"

"Because you're mean to me."

"I don't think I'm that mean," Austen says as he slides over so that I have room.

"You're a bully."

"Hmm, maybe you're just too sensitive."

Before I can respond, Austen is snoring. How am I supposed to sleep with him lying next to me?

Chapter Nine

Austen's chest rises slightly, then drops, then rises again. His steady breathing is intoxicating. I lay beside him, careful not to touch him. There is no room on this tiny bed and half my body is hanging over the edge.

What is going on with me? First, I enjoy kissing him, now I am watching him sleep? He was spot on with that Creeper nickname.

I use this opportunity to look at Austen. When he sleeps, he is not so bad. His soft lips are parted slightly, his well-defined cupid's bow creating a pouty look, his eyelashes are long, his hair disheveled. The sun is peeking through my window and a sliver of light runs across his face illuminating the slight freckling around his nose.

If he were not such a bonehead—he would be glorious.

The sunlight rolls across the rest of his face, crossing the ridge of his nose and finally spreading onto his eyelids, forcing him to wake up.

He blinks, his hazel eyes are desperate to focus. He is confused.

"Where am I?"

"You came into my room last night and fell asleep."

"Oh, it's you."

Austen sits up abruptly, checking to make sure he still has his clothes on.

"We didn't do anything, did we?"

"Other than make out in a closet?"

"That I remember, anything else?"

"Well, I thought about taking advantage of you but changed my mind."

"Ha, sure Birdie." Did he just laugh at something I said?

"Why am I in here?"

"I told you, you just came here and insisted on sleeping in my bed."

"Crap. What time is it?"

"Six thirty."

"Oh, okay. What a mess."

"Are you hungover?"

"A little, I have a headache. You?"

"No, I only pretended to drink. I sipped on the same beer all night. I didn't like the taste of it."

"God, you're weird."

"I know."

"You're not obsessed with me now, are you? I mean, more than you already were?"

"Of course not. I hate to disappoint you, but your kiss wasn't even that memorable. I have had better." Lies and more lies.

"Whatever, I'm a great kisser."

"Eh."

"Well, you weren't exactly great either."

"What did I do wrong?" I can tell by the look on Austen's face he was not expecting this.

"Are you serious?"

"Yeah, I wanna know."

"I was just saying that to be a dick. I didn't mean it, it was fine."

"Oh . . . could I do anything better though?"

"More tongue."

"You would say that."

Austen is rubbing the sleep out of his eyes and stretching. I calm my desire to run my hand up his shirt as he exposes his stomach.

"Don't start getting any funny ideas, Austen. This sleepover was a one-time thing and only out of the goodness of my heart."

"Yeah, yeah. Later, Birdie."

Austen hops out of the bed and out the door, leaving me longing for him to come back. What the hell is wrong with me?

~~~

The air is thick, too thick. Tired of trying to sleep while sweating, I tear the sheets off my sticky body and get up. I cannot stand the heat when I am sleeping. It just so happens that the dungeon is the only part of the house that gets too hot in the summer, the lower level remaining impervious to the air conditioning. The small window above my bed will not open, refusing air entry into this dark space. Too hot to put my robe on, I sulk out of my room and head to the kitchen in a tank top and underwear.

I open the refrigerator and stand in front of it with the door wide open, basking in the coldness. Lifting the hair off the back of my neck, I begin to feel human again.

Thump.

Another thump. A distant voice.

What the heck was that?

I shut the fridge and tiptoe to the door, opening it just a crack to see into the hallway leading to the large dining room. I arch my head back looking up to see if there is anybody at the top of the staircase that leads to Austen's room. I know his room is up there, but I have never been inside it. It has a large *Don't come in here for any reason* sign taped to it and I recognize his handwriting from our biology assignment.

There is a faint light on; Austen's door is open slightly.

What is he doing?

I inch my way out into the dining room so I can get a

better view when hushed whispers become apparent.

"I need to get home. Aiesha is going to find out if I don't get home soon."

"Is that a problem?"

"Yes, I don't want her to know about us. I don't want anybody to know about us. The fewer people who know, the better."

Austen sounds pained, "Why are you so embarrassed to be sleeping with me?"

"You just wouldn't understand. Just let me go, I'll see you later."

"Whatever."

I flatten against the wall so that Liza does not see me as she sprints down the stairs.

Liza and Austen. I know he said they were sleeping together, but I did not really believe it, convincing myself she was too cool to sleep with the likes of him.

A sinking sensation begins to overwhelm my insides, wreaking havoc on my stability.

I prop myself up against the wall, but it is not enough to keep me upright and I stumble onto the floor.

"Who's there?" Austen heard. *Shit.*

"Sorry, it's Birdie."

"Get up here."

I reluctantly head up the stairs then hide my lower half behind the doorframe of his room. Austen is shirtless again, sitting on the edge of the bed. Soft lighting and music create an ambiance I assume was meant for sex. Not that I would know.

"What the hell are you doing creeping around, Birdie?"

"I was too hot in my room, so I went to the fridge to cool down. I didn't mean to overhear anything."

"What'd you overhear?"

"That you're sleeping with Liza and that she doesn't

want anyone to know."

"Ugh Birdie, you need to announce yourself next time, don't just listen to my conversations."

"Sorry . . . why doesn't she want anyone to know?"

"I don't know. Women are difficult."

"Are you guys serious?"

"I don't think so, I like her, but I don't think she likes me all that much."

"But you're having sex."

"Yeah, but that doesn't mean it's serious." Oh, it would to me.

"Why are you hiding behind there?"

"I'm only in my underwear."

"Oh okay, can I ask you something and you won't judge me?"

"Sure," I say as I slide into his room and grab a pillow to cover my lower half.

"Am I a bad kisser?"

"Why do you ask? I thought you said you were a great kisser."

"Well, Liza sleeps with me but she doesn't like to kiss me . . . I don't know, I just thought maybe I was bad at it or something."

"I wouldn't know."

"What do you mean, we kissed."

"I know but I don't have anything to compare it to."

Austen's eyes are wide, "I thought you said you'd kissed other people before."

"I lied."

"Why?"

"I didn't want you to think I was lame."

"Oh," Austen is rubbing the back of his neck now as if trying to figure out what to say.

"Why haven't you kissed anyone?"

"I've avoided it. One of my foster sisters told me once

to never fall in love because it makes it so much harder when we have to move away. Plus, it just ends eventually, all good things do, so it's better to avoid the pain."

"Real dark even for you, Birdie. How many foster homes have you lived in?"

"At least eight since my parents died."

"Wow, I've only ever lived in this house. Well here and the condo in the city. I stay there when I'm in school . . . I would've done better if I had known it was your first kiss."

Something is coming over me, it may be the music, it may be the soft lighting, it may be the bare chest next to me, but I have an overwhelming sensation to kiss Austen again. His lips are parted slightly, and he is looking at me with intensity. I think he might be feeling the same.

"Was I okay at it?"

"Hm?"

"At kissing?" I bite my lip nervously.

"You needed to move your lips more, and you didn't do anything with your tongue."

"I guess I don't know what to do with it."

"Want me to show you?" God, yes. Geez, *calm down,* Birdie.

"Okay."

Austen leans in, taking a deep breath before his lips touch mine.

He whispers into my mouth, "Like this," then gently caresses his tongue against mine. I mimic with my tongue and his soft moan is my reward. After a beat, Austen stops and leans back, looking at me confused.

"Sorry, we shouldn't be doing this . . . I don't know what is going on with Liza and I don't want to mess it up."

"You're right. Me neither, she's, my friend. Plus,

you're my archnemesis and I hate you."

"I'm your archnemesis?"

"Yeah, of course."

Austen laughs then says, "You are one strange bird."

Chapter Ten

Why is it tense now?

Tension fills my pores whenever I see Austen, awkwardness prevailing. We have not spoken one word to each other in the two weeks since we kissed but when I see him, my body tenses in an unbearable way.

What does it mean? And how can I make it stop?

What is even stranger is that on several occasions I have even spotted him looking at me. This has never happened before; he has always either seen right through me or failed to see me at all. He has never *intentionally* looked at me. While we may not be speaking to each other, he has been nicer in that he has not blatantly given me a hard time. I guess this is an improvement.

It is July tenth, and I am deep into my millionth reading of *Pride and Prejudice* when a quiet tapping is at my door. It is after eleven and I know it is not Liza or Aiesha, so my brain immediately goes to Austen.

Maybe I misheard.

Tap, tap.

Okay, maybe not.

I get up and open the door, cautiously.

"Austen? What're you doin' here?"

Austen sighs a long sigh, then holds up a bottle of Moscato, "Do you like this stuff?"

"Oh, I don't know. I've never had it."

"Girls love it . . . can I come in?"

"I guess." The tension is building.

"What're you doing in here?"

"Reading."

"What book?"

"*Pride and Prejudice*, it's my favorite."

"Why do you like it so much?"

Austen is sitting on the edge of my bed, so I crawl up

beside him and watch him take a swig out of the wine bottle.

"Lots of reasons but mostly because it reminds me of my mother."

"Was it her favorite, too?"

I gulp down the sweet wine, surprising myself with how much I like it.

"Yeah, she named me Elizabeth after the lead character." This is true. When I moved in with my adoptive parents at the age of five, I had another name, one that was originally given to me by the staff at the adoption agency I went through—after I was found at the train station. They named me Jane. As in Jane Doe. My adoptive mother Carol wanted me to have a real name so she asked me if would like to be called Elizabeth. I loved it, so they had my name legally changed to Elizabeth Wright when they formally adopted me.

"Oh, wow, you weren't kidding, she really did love that book."

"I've read it a million times. I always read it on July tenth, my mother's birthday. So, why'd you stop by?"

Please stay slips through my consciousness, mortifying me.

"I don't know, was just bored and wanted to talk to someone. Do you wanna be alone with your book since it is your mother's birthday and all?"

"Another moment of human decency from Austen Markey. Amazing."

Austen rolls his eyes, "Shut up."

~~~

Thirty minutes and one empty bottle later, we are laughing. Austen and I, laughing together. This is surreal.

"You know, you're not nearly as bad as I thought you

were, Birdie."

"Why did you hate me so much in high school?"

"I didn't hate you. I just bullied you. I don't know why I am such a dick sometimes. I guess I do it for attention or something. At least that is what my therapist says. You were an easy target."

"How so?"

"You were the new kid coming into the last semester of high school. Do you know how abnormal that is? The only other new kid we had in our class was sophomore year and he was an exchange student from Italy. Plus, you dropped your stuff all over on the first day. So, like I said, an easy target."

"You shouldn't pick on people like that, Austen, it makes life so much harder."

"I know, I'm not proud of it. It was part of this popular image I had created for myself. Now that high school is over, I'm not sure what the point was."

"So, you think I'm cool now?"

"Sure, now I can see that you're pretty chill. Although cool is a stretch. You're a bit nerdy. I mean you hang out here most nights, I assume just reading. Plus, you're one of the strangest girls I have ever met."

"What's wrong with reading? Don't you read?"

"Nothing is wrong with it, usually it just means you aren't partying. I don't read unless I have to."

"What do you like to do, other than float in the pool and party?" I say as I take another swig.

"I don't really know. I hang out with my friends and I like to work out. Other than that, I don't know if I am all that interesting."

"How are things going with Liza?"

"Nothing is going on. I don't think she really likes me."

"Why do you say that?"

"She is so hot and cold. Late at night, she is all over me but when I see her during the day, she ignores me and won't respond to my texts. I'm starting to think she is seeing someone else." The thought of Austen's dad pops into my head, but I do not think it is my business to say anything to him.

"Why are you with someone who treats you that way?"

"I don't know. I have liked her for years. She is a little older and smoking hot. I can't help it."

"But you're rich and popular, you could have anyone."

"Could I have you?" My heart stops. What?

"Um, you're not my type." Lies.

"What's your type, Birdie? Smart nerdy guys?"

"Probably."

"You don't find me attractive? Most girls do."

I roll my eyes, "I don't find your ego attractive."

"Ha, fair. What 'bout my face and body?"

"Why do you care if I find you attractive? You barely notice me, why would you care if I was into you or not?"

"Are you saying you're into me?" Austen's left eyebrow arches slightly, my instincts tell me to run but the wine is making me tingly and brave. I reach over and place my hand on Austen's cheek. "Not. At. All."

Austen laughs then his eyes go wide. His facial expression changes and before I know it, his lips are on mine, timid but hopeful. His warm tongue slides in, reminding me of what he said so I reciprocate, mimicking his movements. My heart begins to beat so hard that my body flushes, my breathing is erratic.

Austen moves his hand underneath my shirt and bra, stroking my breast, "Is this okay?"

"Yes," I say into his mouth, displaying my eagerness.

I lay back on my bed, Austen places one hand on each side of me, hovering as he begins to kiss my neck and down my chest. He runs a hand along the inside of my jeans, feeling my underwear underneath. Leaning back on his heels, he slowly undoes the button of my jeans, unzipping them slightly.

"I need to tell you something," my body is shaking with nerves.

"What?" Austen stops pulling my jeans down so that I can speak.

"I've never done this before."

Austen looks confused, crinkling his brows together, "Done what?"

"Had sex."

"I know, Birdie, I mean I figured that when you said you had never kissed anyone before."

"Is that bad?"

Austen zips my pants back up, buttoning them before laying down by my side, leaning on one arm. He has an uneasiness about him now.

"No, not bad . . . I've just never been with a virgin before."

"Wouldn't you prefer someone who knows what they're doing?"

"Not necessarily, I think it could be kinda hot."

This intrigues me, "Hot?"

"Yeah, but I would feel kind of guilty about it."

"Why?"

"Well, I don't want to take your virginity and you get the wrong idea."

"What idea is that?"

"That we're a couple or something." Oh. I can feel my heart settle into my stomach.

"Oh, I see, does that mean we have to stop?" *Please do not stop*, I beg internally.

"We don't have to, but I wasn't planning on taking any virginities tonight."

"Isn't this what you came here for?" Austen bites down on his lower lip, revealing a bashful side. He just keeps surprising me.

"To be honest, no. I've been thinking about you a lot since that night we kissed in my room. I just wanted to spend some time with you, I never thought you'd be interested in sleeping with me and definitely not tonight."

"But you said I was gross."

Austen looks at me with surprise, "Did I? I'm sorry I said that, Birdie. You're not gross at all. Okay, don't use this against me, Birdie, but I actually think you're quite beautiful."

Nobody has ever told me I was beautiful. I sit up and crawl on top of him, straddling him at his waist. I bend down and kiss his cheek, then the other, until I land at his lips. I give him my best attempt at a kiss, hoping that I am doing it right. I think I am starting to get the hang of this, and the slight moan reassures me that I am on the right track.

A couple of glorious minutes later I pull back, breaking the kiss.

"This is not a good idea. I mean, Liza is my friend, and if you two are an item I don't want to be the one you cheat with."

"We've never said we're exclusive, so cheating is not something I need to worry about."

"I know, but still. I feel guilty."

"Okay, fair enough. I'll go. I'm hoping that Liza comes around, so I better not screw it up. I'll see you later," Austen hops off the bed and leaves the room, taking my heart with him.

Chapter Eleven

I have come to my senses. My fleeting stray into madness is over. I am not now, nor will I ever be interested in Austen Markey. Not really anyway. My moment of weakness simply resulted from a lifetime of singledom and nothing more. Plus, he called me beautiful and that ended up being more powerful than I thought. I spend the next couple of days convincing myself that I am over this silly crush.

This realization comes, in part, thanks to Aiesha's brother, Malcolm. The morning after my moment of weakness with Austen, Aiesha texts me a picture of her brother with a heart emoji. She is trying to play matchmaker and it is working.

Today at lunch, Aiesha gives me all the details on her brother just like she promised.

"Birdie, he is the sweetest guy ever and he's so cute. You two would hit it off, I just know it."

"Am I his type though? He seems way out of my league."

"Don't be ridiculous, you're awesome, don't ever let anyone tell you differently."

"If he is up for a date, of course, I'm into it."

"Great, you will not regret this. Why are you being so quiet, Liza?" Liza has not mentioned Austen or Heath at any of our lunches lately, but I wonder if that is what is on her mind.

"I have news."

"Oh god, girl, what?" Aiesha suspects the worst.

"I slept with Heath again."

"WHY?"

"He is so hot."

"You're crazy."

"Austen caught us."

Aiesha is panicking, "WHAT? How did he catch you? Is he going to tell his mom?" My heart is pounding now.

"No, he would never. He is more upset about it because he is like obsessed with me. He walked in on me servicing his dad on my knees." The image is now burned into my brain.

"Austen has been into you for years, Liza, that's no surprise. I'm sure he was disturbed, but at least he isn't going to tell his mom and hopefully, he is over you by now."

"Welllll . . . now that you mention it."

"NO."

"Yes."

"He's still into you? How do you know?"

"I have been hooking up with him for the past couple of months."

"WHAT." I act like I am just as surprised as Aiesha whose jaw has dropped.

"Yeah, but don't worry, I'll end things with Austen. I want to keep seeing Heath. I want a man not a boy."

"You're wild. If you're not careful you're going to get yourself fired."

"I know. Don't tell anyone. Birdie, will you keep it a secret?"

"I won't say a word to anyone." Crap. Poor Austen.

~~~

I have just finished mopping the kitchen floor and race back to my dungeon to prepare for my date with Malcolm. He is going to pick me up and take me to Charlie's, a cheap but famously delicious pizza place. By the looks of his picture and the description from Aiesha, I am in for a treat. He just graduated high school and is apparently 'sweet as pie.' I just hope he is as handsome in real life as he is in his pictures.

I tear off my grubby clothes and opt for the Nirvana t-shirt Aiesha let me borrow and pull my stringy hair back into a loose braid. Fairly satisfied, I grab my lip balm and wallet and sprint to the front entrance to wait for Malcolm.

I sit on the stone steps, attempting to look cool and sexy at the same time, the possibilities of romance are making my heart flutter. I am not looking for love or anything serious, but I would like a few experiences under my belt before heading to college.

This is my first official date. I do not even know what to do or say on a date. I rehearse some questions I looked up online earlier today and just hope he likes me.

"What're you doing?" I jolt in response.

"Oh geez, you scared me. I'm waiting for my date." Austen gives me a confused face—so I continue, "Is that so hard to believe?"

"I guess not. I just thought you were too obsessed with me to go on a date with someone else." Austen sits on the stones next to me, running his hands through his perfect hair.

"I'm not obsessed with you. We just kissed a couple of times, right? Besides, you were the one who told me that you didn't want to date me."

"I know and I don't. Who is this guy anyway?" Austen is biting his lower lip, making me want to kiss him again.

"Malcolm."

"Aiesha's brother?"

"Yeah, why? Do you know him?"

"Yeah, he's cool. I just don't think you're his type."

"What's that supposed to mean?"

"Don't get all offended. I just mean I don't think he is into quirky, nerdy girls."

Crap, my fluttering heart is starting to worry that this

was a bad idea.

"Oh, well, Aiesha set us up. He hasn't met me. He probably won't be into me."

"HA, a blind date? That's hilarious."

"Why?"

"I just think we are too young for blind dates."

"Is there an age requirement?"

"No, but there should be. Where are you two going for this date?"

"He's taking me to Charlie's in the city."

"That is a bit of a distance. Is there no food near here that he likes or something?"

A beat-up green Subaru pulls into the circular stone drive, a face peering out. It is Malcolm, and he is even more handsome than his pictures. If you look up the definition of tall, dark, and handsome in the dictionary, it would just have a picture of him. I stand up quickly, wishing I were someone else, someone way cooler, and open the car door.

"Hi, you must be Malcolm."

"Hey Birdie, hop in," Malcolm says with a surprisingly deep voice considering his age. He waves briefly to Austen before putting the car in drive.

"Are you friends with Austen?"

"No, I wouldn't call us friends. He used to be my mortal enemy, now he is just a regular enemy."

"Oh, I see," Malcolm says laughing. His perfect teeth shining.

"Hope you like pizza."

"Absolutely," I say while simultaneously reminding myself to be cool. I glance in the side view mirror and see Austen standing with his hands shoved in his pockets and a look of annoyance on his face.

What does he have to be annoyed about?

~~~

Charlie's is a well-lit classic pizza parlor. The type of place you think of when you think of New York. The workers even have thick Italian accents, further adding to the genuine vibe. Malcolm and I find a booth in the back corner, the checkered print tablecloth solidifying my belief that this will be a great pizza.

"Have you ever been here before?"

"No, I've walked past it many times though and have heard people talk about it."

"Well, it's my favorite. They have the best New York-style pizza you can get."

"Can't wait," I say this as I nervously play with the loose strand of hair that has fallen from my braid.

"Listen, I don't normally do this blind date thing but my sister raves about you and thinks we'd hit it off."

"No problem, I don't do this kind of thing either." Never.

A man with too hairy of arms comes over, "We have special cheese pizza tonight. I will bring it out to you."

"Okay, thanks, Antonio." After the man leaves, Malcolm explains, "Always get the special. Otherwise, they get grumpy." We both laugh.

"Hey, Malcolm," says a skinny, dark-haired young man.

"Hey, Marcus. How're you?"

"Good, I didn't know you were going to come in tonight."

"Yup, I wanted to bring my date. This is Birdie, Birdie this is Marcus." I smile up to Marcus who does not reciprocate my friendly expression.

"So, you bring dates here now?"

"Yeah, is that a problem?"

"No, I don't care." Marcus walks off in a huff and I

am left very confused.

"Who's that guy Malcolm, a friend of yours? He didn't seem very happy to see you here."

"Oh, it's nothing, just ignore him. Let's talk about you."

I'm more nervous around Malcolm than I care to admit. His presence is undeniable, his face unbeatable. I hope that I am not just a pity date because if I have even the slightest chance with this human, I would do anything to make it happen. Sell an organ? Sure. Push a boulder to the top of a mountain? No problem. Ride the scariest roller coaster in the world? Done.

He is way better than that Austen guy. He is not rude, he does not call me Creeper, and he is not some pretentious spoiled rich kid who has never vacuumed a day in his life. I shake my head as I think this, annoyed that Austen is making space in my brain at all. It was just a couple of kisses. It did not mean anything. Yes, he is the only boy I have ever kissed, but maybe after tonight, that will change.

Chapter Twelve

Charlie's is the first of three dates that week and every time Malcolm asks me for another date, I am surprised. I keep waiting for the shoe to drop and for him to say "just kidding" or to forget about my existence entirely. We usually hang out around the house for these dates, watching movies in my room, talking and laughing.

Everything sounds perfect, right? Something does not feel right, though, as my anxiety about Malcolm not being attracted to me grows in the back of my mind. While we have a great time together, or at least I think we do, Malcolm never does the one thing I want him to: kiss me. So tonight, will be the night. I have rented *Die Hard*, guys love that movie, and I have decided to take the lead and kiss him myself. With just the right amount of makeup on, thanks to Aiesha's help, and another borrowed hipster t-shirt, I am ready for this.

Kissing Malcolm is important for many reasons. First, I want to and second, I do not want to go to college with only one boy kissed under my belt. I need more experience before I embark on such an adventure. I need to know what I am doing so I can kiss college boys with confidence.

It is seven-thirty and there is a light knock. I rush over, try to calm myself with a deep breath, then pull open the door. Darn, it's Austen.

"What're you doing here? Get out of here, I'm waiting for Malcolm."

"I won't be here long. Just wanted to see how things were going with him."

"It's none of your business. Why do you even care anyway?"

"I don't, I'm just bored. Has he kissed you yet?"

"Of course, he has. What kind of question is that?"

"Really?"

"Well, no, but he will tonight."

"You should know that there have been rumors about Malcolm."

"What kind of rumors?"

"That he's gay."

"What? No way, he's not gay. If he were gay, why would he keep asking me out?"

"Maybe because he doesn't want to appear gay. Or maybe because you remind him of a dude."

"No, don't be like that. He's not gay. He likes me." Right?

"How would you know? Has he said that to you?"

"Um, no I guess not."

"Whatever Birdie, good luck with your gay boyfriend." Austen saunters off, clearly proud of himself. He is crazy, Malcolm cannot be gay. At least I do not think so. Of course, I have no clue how I could tell if he is. I cannot ask him about it, that would be so embarrassing.

"Don't bother me tonight, by the way, I have a date over and I don't plan on it being PG like your night is going to be." Austen looks back at me with a side-eye that is the most douchey thing I have ever seen him do.

"Ew. Poor girl!"

Austen smiles at this, leaving me to ponder who his date is. Is it Liza?

~~~

A deep pulsing is in my ears. I think it is blood. My heart is beating so hard that the veins in my head are about to burst. Malcolm appears undisturbed, his calm demeanor only worsening the throbbing in my ears. Malcolm laughs, the current scene in Die Hard must be amusing but I am far too distracted to even notice. I must kiss him. I want to kiss him. I do not want a relationship or love, what I want is experience. Love is something that withers with time or dies abruptly in a car crash. No, what I want is to kiss the boy next to me.

It is time.

"Malcolm?"

"Yeah, Birdie?"

"Can I kiss you?" Please say yes. Malcolm's eyes go wide, and he leans back a little, his surprise surprising me.

"Sure, Birdie."

I lean in towards him slowly, praying to the gods of sex that I kiss this boy right. My lips land on his. It is unexpected. While the mechanics seem right, it does not feel the same as kissing Austen. It seems to be missing that magic I was wanting. We stop after a beat, Malcolm looking unsure.

"Was that okay, Birdie?"

"Yeah, it was very nice. I'm sorry, I have not kissed too many boys before. I might not be doing it right."

"No, you are. It's not you, Birdie . . . I am not sure how to say this, but I'm bi-sexual."

"Oh. What does that mean exactly?"

"It means I like boys, too."

"Oh, but you also like girls?"

"I like you."

I blush, "I like you, too." Right?

~~~

Malcolm leaves my room around ten, a goodbye kiss on the cheek being the only other action I get that night. Disheartened by the PG level of my night, I decided to see what rated R things Austen is up to.

I glide quietly down the hall and up the stairs until I am hovering outside of Austen's door. Am I going to do this? Am I going to eavesdrop? What if he catches me? What if he opens the door and I am just standing there forever solidifying my creeper status?

I tiptoe to the door and rest my ear to it. Music is playing and I hear murmuring. Are they having sex? Flattening more against the door, I can make out bits of what is being said.

"What is it, Liza? I thought you liked me. Why do you come here and sleep with me if you don't like me?"

Liza? How could she do this to him? And with his dad of all people?

"I do like you, Austen, but it's just for fun. I'm not looking for a relationship with you, you're too young for me."

"But you're looking for a relationship with my dad? Are you serious? Because you like how old he is?"

"Your dad and I only slept together a couple of times, Austen, it's not a big deal." Oh yes, it is.

"He's my dad. Do you understand how messed up that is?"

"You're making this a bigger ordeal than it needs to be."

"I don't think I can do this anymore unless you promise to stay away from my dad."

"Well, I can't promise that."

"Whatever, Liza, get out." Oh no, I have got to get out of here. I quickly slide to the side of the door, wanting nothing more than the power of invisibility, the same power that I have always wished for.

The door flies open, light pours onto the floor in front of it. I do not breathe or make a sound. *Please don't see me, please don't see me.* Liza dashes down the stairs, leaving the door open in her wake. Unable to move for fear of being caught, I stay in the same position for what feels like an eternity. The music in the room comes to an end, and I expect Austen to come and shut the door, freeing me from my hold. However, he does not come to the door right away. Instead, I hear a faint sound and I recognize it immediately. He is crying. It is a soft cry, but the sniffling gives it away. Damn, he has feelings? I would never have guessed.

Why is he crying over Liza? The question settles in my chest as a deeper thought pushes its way up to the surface, *I wish he felt that strongly about me.*

Chapter Thirteen

Do I want Austen to care about me? Why? Maybe I just want him to want me, therefore vindicating my damaged pride. The thing I should do is use this information about him crying against him. Humiliate him with it. My desire to embarrass him as he has embarrassed me is strong, but not strong enough, as I never mention it to him or anyone. Instead, I spend the next couple of days berating myself for not being more vindicative, believing somehow that life would be better if I were.

I lay on my bed after a long day working, Austen's face and lips running around my head like an obnoxious child, leaving me wondering why it's Austen's face and not Malcolm's when I hear a tapping at my door. Malcolm is busy tonight, so I know it is not him. God, I hope it is not Austen. I do not seem to know how to act around him. I open the door a crack, peeking out to see a somber face in front of me.

"Can I talk to you?" Austen looks like a dog that has been kicked too many times. I am familiar with the feeling.

"Sure," I say as I open my bedroom door. Austen walks in with trepidation, and I have the sudden fear that he knows I was outside his door the other night.

"What's up?"

"Are you seeing Malcolm tonight?"

"No, he has plans with a friend of his."

"Listen, can you be honest with me?"

"Okay."

"I heard a noise outside of my room the other night when I was with Liza. That wasn't you, was it?"

Shit balls.

"No," I squeak.

71

"Birdie?"

"Okay, yes."

"Why?"

"Well, I was curious about your supposed rated R evening."

"What'd you hear?"

"Not much."

Austen looks at me with scrunched eyebrows, so I go for the truth, "I heard that she's hooking up with your dad and that you asked her to leave unless she stops, and then I heard you cry after she left."

Austen rubs the back of his neck, and I spot a slight shaking in his hand, "Please keep this between us, Birdie. I have an image to maintain and crying is not part of that."

I am blushing, hard. I was not prepared for a genuine Austen, "Okay Austen, I won't tell anyone. Why were you crying over her? You shouldn't let her get to you like that."

"I don't know, I think I am just mortified that she would choose my dad over me. He's always doing this, sleeping with everyone. He used to hook up with all my babysitters, basically any female who is at least eighteen and steps foot in this house is not safe. I wish he'd stop. It's so gross. I hate the guy."

"I don't blame you, that's horrifying." I am not great at comforting people.

"Take it as a warning, Birdie. Avoid him at all costs. He'd be all over you."

"I doubt that. I am not exactly hot like Liza."

"You're hotter than you think, Birdie." I shrug in disbelief.

"Ya know, we could hook up." Austen is smiling and I can't tell if he is serious or not.

I laugh, "Why would I wanna do that?"

"I dunno, experience?"

"Experience?"

"Yeah, do you really wanna go to college a virgin?"

I consider this, "Maybe not, but why would you want to do it?"

"Liza would be so jealous."

"Wow, you're so mature."

"Eh, what do you think?"

"Hmm, well, okay, I guess." What did I just agree to?

"What?"

"I said okay."

"You know, you keep surprising me, Birdie." Is that a good thing?

"When do we do this, NOW?"

"Ha, no. I have to be somewhere. What 'bout later tonight? Midnight?"

"Fine."

"Fine, meet me in my room. Also, don't become too obsessed with me afterward."

I roll my eyes dramatically, "Okay, I will try to refrain from falling for the king of douches."

Austen laughs and walks out of my room and seems normal as he does it. I am anything but normal. My arms are heavy, my legs weak. What the hell did I just agree to?

~~~

Sitting in the bathtub staring at my naked body, I suddenly realize that I have no idea how to prepare for sex. What do I need to do? Do I shave? The few pornographic images I have seen in my life have all been of women without any body hair, so I guess this is what I need to do. I grab my dull, hardly used, years old razor, and attempt to shave my privates. After a couple of painful nicks, I give up. Hopefully, Austen does not notice or care.

I have no idea what I am doing but I hope this is the right choice. Maybe losing your virginity should be treated like ripping off a Band-aid, just hurry up and get it over with. For Austen, this is a simple act of desperation, an attempt to seek revenge as he is a scorned lover. He is willing to sleep with me for the mere possibility that Liza will care. Of course, I know that she will not. Liza told me last week that she finds Austen annoying and pathetic, and she is now only interested in what she calls "Real men." I guess Austen's dad is a real man in her mind, but in mine, he is a dirty old cheater. What's the appeal in that?

I dry off with my towel and quickly braid my hair. I don't own a blow dryer so a braid will have to do for now. I do not own a lot of things, the few belongings I have fitting into a black trash bag and the only thing that matters to me is my mother's worn copy of *Pride and Prejudice*. I slip on a clean pair of flower-patterned underwear, suddenly wishing I owned underwear that was more grown-up. I grab my trusty Nirvana t-shirt that I keep 'forgetting' to return to Aiesha.

Aiesha. I cannot tell her about this. She will be upset because of Malcolm. She will surely find out from Liza though. Maybe I have not thought this through. I do not want to lose the only two friends I currently have. Then again, I will be in Alfred soon and I am sure that Liza and Aiesha will never think of me again.

An undercurrent of stress is building and pushing against the top layer of my skin threatening to burst through, completely tearing me apart. I am going to have sex with Austen. Austen who thinks little of me and whom I hate. I hope it is not terrible, although I do not have anything to compare it to. It is now eleven forty-five. Time for me to make my way to his room. I hope he has not changed his mind. I slip on my sandals and inch my way out of the room up to Austen's. Taking slow steps, trying desperately to calm my beating heart.

The darkness of the house is intercepted by streams of light from the full moon sneaking in through the windows. The only other light can be seen under Austen's bedroom door. He must be in there, waiting for me.

I knock lightly on his door, a quick "Come in" can be heard from the inside. I push the door open and step inside, the soft light from his bedroom lamp illuminating the room only slightly, leaving the corners dark. In true Austen fashion, there is music playing. It is a song I have never heard.

"It's Jessie Ware. Chicks love it." Oh, I can see why as her soft voice fills the room with a sensuous ambiance. I am way out of my league here.

"I'm nervous," I blurt, very uncool like.

"Okay. Just come sit down. You don't need to be nervous." I sit by Austen on his bed, he has on a dark blue t-shirt and jeans. He looks glorious.

"I don't know how to do this."

"You don't have to do much, Birdie. I will take the lead. You can just relax. Here, I brought you a glass of wine."

I sip on the cold, sweet wine, hoping the liquid will transform me into a different, more grown-up person. Austen is looking at me with intensity, but also something else. Is he nervous too?

"Are you sure you wanna do this, Birdie? It's okay if you don't. If you ever need to stop, just tell me. It's no problem, even if it is during and you want to stop, don't hesitate to tell me."

"Okay, thanks. Yes, I am sure. Are you sure?"

Austen nods.

Austen and I sip on our wine for a few minutes, or possibly just a couple of seconds? I no longer have any concept of time.

"I'm going to kiss you now, okay?"

"Okay."

Austen leans in and puts his finger under my chin, lifting me to meet his lips and I feel like I might die of bliss. The sweetness of the wine on his tongue is magical as I could kiss him for days. He breaks away, pushing me down onto the bed, kissing my neck.

"Let's get this shirt off of you."

He pulls the bottom of the shirt over my head, "You must really love Nirvana."

"I've never heard a single song of theirs. I just know that they are cool and from the 90s."

Austen smiles and I melt further into the bed, "You're one strange girl, Birdie."

Don't fall in love. Don't fall in love. Don't fall in love. I repeat this mantra over and over in my head, hoping that somehow it will prevent me from doing the one thing I know will only make my life harder. I cannot fall for Austen. He is not interested in dating me. This is just a one-time thing. I will be in college soon and I will avoid him.

Austen removes my bra and I realize he is the first boy to ever see my chest. I don't have a clue what my breasts should or should not look like. Are they nice? Are they too small? Do they look normal? The clenched jaw on Austen tells me they are doing something for him. The hardening against my leg assures it.

Crap. This is really happening. *Crap.* I don't think I can let it. It suddenly dawns on me that maybe this is more special than I thought. Maybe losing my virginity to someone who does not like me is not actually how I want to do this. My body freezes and Austen notices.

"What's wrong?"

"I don't know if I can do this."

"Okay. Did I do something wrong?"

"No, it's not that. I just think that I should give my virginity to someone who likes me. I'm sorry I thought I could do this."

"It's okay Birdie, you don't have to apologize. I get it." Austen sits up and hands me my bra and shirt.

I sit up and put my bra and shirt back on, Austen looking away to give me privacy.

"You know, I don't dislike you, Birdie. I know I was mean to you in the beginning, but you're not so bad. Do you still think of me as your enemy?"

I smile, "I want to, but you make it difficult for me. You were my mortal nemesis but became just a regular enemy. How about I downgrade you from regular enemy or sort of enemy?"

"Sure, Birdie."

"Can you stop calling me Creeper?"

"Haven't you noticed? I haven't called you Creeper in ages. Are you done getting dressed yet?"

I pull the bottom of my shirt over my stomach and say, "Yes, I am. Do you want me to leave now?"

"No, why don't you stay, have some wine with me. I don't mind hanging out if you are into it."

"Sure."

Austen and I sit in silence drinking wine as he plays me a few more of Jessie Ware's songs, I think I have a new favorite singer. I try to focus my attention on anything in the room other than his face, the last thing I want is for him to think I like him. *Geez*, my maturity knows no bounds. I smile as I think this.

"What are you smiling about?"

"Oh, nothing. I just like the songs you're playing."

"Give me your phone and I will add them to your playlist for you." It's hilarious that he thinks I have a playlist. How would I even do that?

"Okay," I reach into my pants pocket and give Austen my phone that I got with the forty dollars a month payment plan.

"What's this, Birdie?"

"My phone?"

"Yeah, I've never seen one like this."

"I got it from a corner store, it only cost a hundred dollars and the plan is forty a month. I got it with my first paycheck from working here. It's my first phone. I always had to borrow one."

"You can't be serious. I cannot imagine living without a phone, that's crazy."

"I didn't have a choice."

"Your life has been so different than mine."

"No shit."

Austen looks through my phone like it is a fossil he just dug out of the earth when he says, "I have an old iPhone you can have if you want. I always get the latest iPhones when they are released, and I sell the old ones to my friends for a discount."

"I can't afford a phone of yours."

"It's okay, you can have it."

"Why would you do that?"

"You need a better phone than this Birdie, this is garbage. Trust me, you will love to have a nice phone. Plus, I can set up a sweet playlist for you if you want. Seems like you're pretty clueless about music."

"If you really don't mind. You will just give it to me out of the kindness of your heart? But I thought your heart was black as tar."

"Damn Birdie, I'm not that bad." Austen gets off the bed and goes to his dresser and pulls out an old phone.

"Here you go."

"That's nice of you Austen. Thanks."

"No problem. It doesn't matter to me."

"I don't know anything about phones, but can I use my phone plan with this phone?"

"No idea, you might have to find out. If not, just sell it and keep the cash."

"Okay. As a thank you, I officially downgrade you from sort of enemy to former enemy."

"Great, maybe one day you can upgrade me to friend."

"Don't hold your breath." Austen's hazel eyes light up with laughter at this. He thinks I am pretty funny which is one of the few things he has probably ever been right about.

Chapter Fourteen

Over the next few nights, I dream of Austen. I imagine his hazel eyes on me, piercing my soul, tugging every fiber of my being towards him. When I am awake, I reassure myself that it is just a crush, a simple, silly crush that will fade away as all crushes do (at least so I've heard) and I trek on spending my days cleaning and my nights with Malcolm.

Malcolm is the sweetest. He brings over snacks for movie nights and holds my hand gently as we talk about our likes and dislikes. He texts me during the days, telling me he has been thinking about me and cannot wait to see me later. His sweetness is something that I do not want to take for granted, however, I cannot help but find it slightly predictable and boring. Besides the one shared kiss and the handholding, Malcolm and I do not have any physical contact. I am no expert, but I am starting to find it a bit strange. I am beginning to wonder if he is keeping something from me.

It is noon on a Wednesday, so I know Aiesha and Liza are outside getting ready for lunch, so I prop my broom up against the wall and head outside to meet up with them. I open the secret back entrance out to the garden. I say secret because only the help use it and it was built to be unnoticed. Beams of sunlight strike my face, settling heat into my pores. I wish I were not wearing my black jeans today but when you only own a couple of pairs of jeans you run out of options quickly. I spot Aiesha and Liza sitting in a new spot, instead of at the horse barn— they are in the garden. They are seated in the grass by the white roses, cross-legged with bright blue and red sunglasses on. They wonder why I do not wear sunglasses outside like I have money for those types of trivialities. I always just respond with something like "I forgot them inside" and change the subject, not wanting to dive too deep into my poorness and the fact that I need to save every penny for supplies for college.

"Hey, Birdie! Over here!" Liza yells out as though I do not see them.

I take my sandals off, letting my feet tread over the freshly mowed grass until I reach them, imitating them by crossing my legs when I sit and noticing a green tint across the bottom of my feet.

"So? How's it going with Malcolm?" Aiesha asks with a raised eyebrow.

"Good, I think. I mean, I've never really dated anyone before, so I don't have anything to compare it to, but he is really sweet."

"Is it getting serious?"

"I don't know. How do you know when it is?" My naivete knows no bounds.

"Well, if you're sleeping together that is one way to know."

"Not really, I mean I sleep with guys all the time and it's never serious," Liza licks chocolate pudding off of her spoon as she says this, and I revel in how sexual she is even when she is just eating.

"We all know about you hooking up Master Heath, Liza, but Birdie isn't the type of girl to have sex with someone she isn't serious about."

Feeling the need to clarify, I say, "We're not sleeping together."

"Why not?" Aiesha seems genuinely surprised.

"I don't think he wants to. I mean, he's never tried."

"Oh," Aiesha says before looking down at the grass, scrunching her eyebrows together like she is thinking about what I said.

"Is that weird?" Now I am nervous.

"Well, a little. I mean most guys tend to go right for

that."

"Maybe he doesn't want to?" Am I repulsive? The gross comment Austen made before resurfacing.

"Why wouldn't he want to, you're adorable." Liza smiles and I almost believe her. "I mean, you're adorable in like a little puppy kind of way. Maybe he doesn't see you as a sex object."

"Don't be mean, Liza, Birdie is sexy, she just doesn't know it yet." I am starting to really dislike Liza.

"Maybe you should ask him. I don't know much about my brother's sex life because, EW, but you should just ask him."

We sit for another thirty minutes as I snack on the bag of chips Liza brought while grappling with my insecurities.

~~~~

It's my turn to pick the movie so I just select a random movie on Netflix, too nervous to give it a lot of thought.

"Cool, this looks good." Malcolm is already eating the cheese puffs he brought, orange dust caked on his fingertips.

Okay, here goes. "Malcolm, can I ask you something?"

"Sure, what's up?" he says, licking the tips of his fingers.

"Are you, are you into me? Or . . . not? I was just wondering because we haven't done anything physical, so I wasn't sure if you liked me like that or not?" This might be the most awkward question I have ever asked another human, well other than the time I had to ask Mrs. Lindstrom, my history teacher, for a towel to wipe up the blood on my seat. Being thirteen and without a mother, I was not prepared for how to handle that time of the month. The horrid realization that blood had seeped through my pants when I was unprepared struck at the worst possible time: right at the end of the first class of the day, leaving me to wear a pair of way too big sweats from the lost and found bin which led to rumors that I had pooped myself for the two months I was at that school. I had never been happier to move to a new foster home in a new school district in my short life.

Malcolm is surprised by my question, which is evident by his cheesy hand hanging in midair and his eyes widening.

"Sorry to ask, I just wasn't sure what was going on with us." I could die right now.

"I like you a lot, Birdie. I know we haven't done much in the physical department but, to be honest, I'm not really sure that is the type of relationship I want."

"Oh, okay."

"It's nothing against you, you are lovely, but, but... I think I'm more interested in men now."

"Oh . . . I see. So, you're gay, not bisexual?"

"I dunno really. I mean, I thought I was bisexual, but I'm starting to think I have a preference."

"Oh. Why've you been hanging out with me then?"

"Please don't be mad, Birdie, but my family has been giving me a hard for not having girlfriends, and—I . . . I just . . . am not ready to tell them I like men."

"So, you're hanging with me to make your parents happy?"

"Kind of, they have been so excited to hear that I'm dating you, I didn't want to let them down, so I've been going along with it. I'm so sorry. I hope you're not mad. I don't want you to feel used or anything."

"No, I'm not mad. I'm kind a relieved, I wasn't feeling the sparks with you either. I kept trying too, though."

"Why?"

"Well, I'd rather like you because you are so sweet and nice to me."

"Rather like me than who?"

"Never mind, I don't wanna say." I chew on my lip nervously.

"I just told you my secret, you can tell me yours and then we'll call it even."

"Don't tell anyone, ever, but . . . okay . . . I'm not proud of this . . . but Austen."

"Really?"

"Yeah, we've kissed a couple of times and we almost had sex one night but didn't, but I hate him, so I have been trying to force myself to like you instead."

"Haha, hate is not the opposite of love, Birdie, I think you might have it bad for him."

"No way, it's just a minor attraction. What do you mean hate is not the opposite of love?"

"Indifference is the opposite of love —not hate. Hate means you feel for that person, you feel a lot for them. People confuse them sometimes. Love and hate I mean."

"Oh, so you're saying that because I hate him, it means I have feelings for him?"

"Sure. It is a famous quote actually, so I can't take credit for it. You know you can't force yourself not to like someone, Birdie, trust me, I've tried." Malcolm's face reflects sadness and I place my hand on his, hoping to offer some comfort.

"Malcolm, you should take your own advice."

He smiles at this, "You're right, I should. Maybe I will start dating someone I want to date, no offense. Can we keep being friends, Birdie?"

"Hell yes. I will take all of the friends I can get, Malcolm. You know I'm kind of surprised to hear that about your parents, I mean Aiesha is basically a hippie and even has a tattoo on the back of her neck."

84

"Yeah, and my parents are NOT happy about it."

"Oh, I see."

"But that doesn't compare to their macho, super athletic, all-star son being gay. They will be so disappointed."

"I'm sorry, Malcolm," I grip Malcolm's hand a little tighter, "I think you're great."

Malcolm smiles, "Thanks, Birdie. I think you're pretty great too."

~~~

Malcolm and I do not even pay attention to whatever movie we were watching on Netflix as we are deep into conversation.

"So, have you ever dated a boy before?"

"No, not really. I have kissed one though. You might remember meeting him at Charlie's. His name is Marcus."

"Is that the grumpy guy who came over to us?"

"Yup, that's him."

"OH my gosh, that explains why he was so cold to me, he was jealous."

"Yeah, he's pretty great and I started going to Charlie's a lot just to see him. Then one day before I finished my pizza, Marcus asked me to take his break with him and sit on a bench behind the restaurant. He said he had some weed, and we could smoke it. When we got back there, though, he said he didn't have any smoke, he just wanted to ask me if I liked him because he liked me."

"That's so sweet, Malcolm."

"I know, I was so nervous, I just nodded and he grabbed me and kissed me. It was a great kiss but I kind of panicked and just ran out. I didn't return until a week later with you. I was trying to send him an 'I'm straight' message."

"Oh no, he must've been heartbroken."

"I know."

"If you like him, you should talk to him, Malcolm. He obviously likes you."

"Yeah, I might. I don't know. Romance is complicated."

"I don't have a ton of experience, or any really, but I believe you." Malcolm and I both laugh, and I realize it is pretty great to have friends.

Chapter Fifteen

Summer nights at the castle are my favorite. The days are too warm and overbearing but sometimes the nights have just the right amount of weight in the sky to be comforting instead of oppressive. I wander around the property, staring at the night sky and the beauty of this old house. The home is grand in the day but has a mystery to it in the dark, reminding me of some elderly lady who comes off as proper and true to her word but has secrets that she will never share. It is only at night when you can get a hint that there is more to the old broad than meets the eye.

Dark shadows from the trees lining the property dance across the large stones that make up the exterior of the castle, the moon casts an eerie glow across the grounds, reflecting off the white roses. Only one manufactured light is in sight; it comes from an old lamp post that rises high above the driveway mimicking the torch from a weary traveler riding in on horseback. I have no idea how old the home is, but I can assume it is from another time thanks to the intricate detail of the lamp post that looks to have been carved by hand and is still beautiful even with its slight fracturing. The cracks only add to its beauty, giving it character.

I have never lived inside a wealthy person's home before so I cannot determine what is good taste versus what is not, but I can tell you that this home casts an air of determination and resilience that I associate with the homes of a time past, reflecting the spirit of a generation long-gone. Some of the decorations are odd, such as statues of fat babies and scary abstract art that makes no sense, but most of it is sublime. The Markey's have a large painting that sits above a fireplace in one of the sitting rooms, it is a soft painting of a log cabin with smoke coming out of the chimney. It is dreamy and breathtaking.

I think about this painting as I sit on the steps in front of the grand entryway and run my finger over the stone column beside me. The harsh but cool sensation of the hard surface is both chilling and welcoming at the same time. I like to sit out here sometimes late at night when the rest of the world is asleep and think about my adoptive parents and the life that could have been. I wonder about what I would be doing at this very moment if they had lived. I think they would have provided a great life for me and my foster siblings. It would not have been nearly as grand as the lives of the Markey's, but I would have loved it.

I do have a certain amount of envy for the type of people who live in places like this. I would be lying if I said I didn't. My adoptive parents and I lived in average surroundings, but we had something that a lot of people do not: love. And lots of it. That is one thing I have noticed about the Markey's, the lack of love. Austen's parents are rarely at the house, usually, they are in the city working, or traveling, and when Austen's dad is here, he barely speaks to Austen but does manage to make time for Liza (if you can call it that). The lack of love is apparent, and I have started to realize that this is why Austen bullied me. He is sad. So, while he may live in this beautiful home, his life is not beautiful. It is better than mine, of course, at least he has never been in the system and has a castle to come home to, but nevertheless, I can recognize that it is not a great life.

That is one of the few things that Austen and I have in common, we are both lacking love from parents. I had an enormous amount of it once but have not come across it since. My foster sister's warning to avoid love at all costs still reverberates in my ear. Even if you are lucky enough to experience it, it will not last. It will fade away just like this perfect summer night. The good news is that without love, the hurt does not hurt as bad. It is the best thing one can do for oneself: avoid love. As I think this, I doubt my own words because even though I do not want to feel the pain of losing someone I love again, I still would not trade the time I had with my adoptive parents for anything. So maybe love makes the pain worth it?

Deep in thought, it takes me a moment to realize that I am not alone. I instinctually look up and see a figure coming towards me. Although it is dark, I am not afraid. This community is very secure, so I assume it is someone who lives here or works here, plus, when you grow up in the system as I did, you become hard to spook. I remain quiet as the figure walks towards me at a quick, slightly uneven pace. As he nears, I can tell he is in a dark hoodie and has his head bent down, staring at the ground, hands shoved in pockets. I doubt he has spotted me. I make a noise by pushing my shoe across the stone, creating a slight rubbing sound. It does the trick and, several feet in front of me, the figure finally looks up.

Austen.

"Oh shit, Birdie? You scared me. I didn't think anyone was out here."

"Sorry, I didn't mean to scare you."

"What're you doing?" Austen is leaning against the stone column now, pulling something out of his pocket.

"I like to come out here sometimes late at night and look up at the stars. It's peaceful. This is the first time in my life I've ever really seen the stars, I hate that you can't see them in the city because they're so wonderful, magical really."

"Are they? I've never really noticed. I was just walking back from a party a few properties down."

"That's the problem with you."

"What?"

"You don't notice things. I bet you don't even notice how beautiful your home is."

"Yeah, it's okay but I have friends with nicer ones."

"Ha, wow, rich kids never appreciate what they have."

"I guess I do sound a little snobby."

"Just a little," I say while rolling my eyes, but it is too dark for him to see, "you should look up at the stars sometimes. It's one of life's greatest joys."

"Really?"

"Really."

"Okay, I will."

"So, how was the party?"

"Boring, that's why I left." Austen has lit the end of a peculiar looking cigarette and it dawns on me that it is probably a joint.

"You want a hit?" He says after he takes a pull and sounds as though he is holding his breath.

"I've never smoked weed before."

"There are a lot of things you haven't done. I would've thought that someone growing up in foster care wouldn't be as sheltered as you."

Sheltered? Am I sheltered? Maybe he is right. I find it ironic that a foster kid who spent the last eight years without a shelter of her own is now being called sheltered, but I keep the irony to myself.

"I always focused on getting good grades and staying invisible as much as I could. I just wanted to get by. Survive. I avoided a lot of social interactions, so maybe that is why I haven't had as many experiences as you." I sound more offended than I really am.

"Well, I didn't mean that to be an insult or anything. I don't think it is a bad thing to be sheltered. I just wonder how you will do in college. Might be a bit of a shock."

"There is not much that can shock me. Although I've

been worried about going to college without more experience. That's why I considered having sex with you the other night, I don't want to be the virgin, the odd one out. I want to fit in, for once in my life." Why am I sharing this with him? Maybe Malcolm was right, and I am into him.

"You worry too much. I bet a lot of people go to college virgins. It's nothing to be worried about. It'll happen when it is right. Although, if you ever change your mind, I'm happy to take care of that for you." Austen smirks as he says this, then takes another puff. I become brave. What the hell.

"Lemme try."

"Okay, but be warned. It can feel weird. Take a long pull, then hold the smoke in for a second or two." I do as I am told, and, within moments, I am deep into a coughing fit.

Austen is laughing, "Nice, Birdie. You're going to feel that. So, how's it going with Malcolm?"

"You'll be happy to know that you were right. He doesn't like me."

"Because he's gay, right?"

"Yes, but you can't say anything to anyone about it. He hasn't told his family yet."

"No problem, I won't say anything. You upset? Did you like him or what?"

"Well, no, not really. I liked him as a friend but there was no real spark."

"Hmm. Hey, you want to go for a walk? Nothing is more fun than exploring while stoned."

"Sure, as long as you promise to look at the stars," I say, way too happy about the offer. God, I'm pathetic.

"Definitely, stargazing while stoned doesn't sound too bad."

~~~

An indiscriminate amount of time later and I am no longer myself. I am not sure what I am saying to Austen, I believe my statements are true and rational, but his laughter tells me they are not. Here is what I do know: the grass is warm on my face and I can no longer feel my ears. I worry I am hallucinating as I see small glowing orbs floating about, drifting in the moonlight.

"What're these little balls of sunshine?"

Austen laughs, "Fireflies, Birdie. Haven't you ever seen them before?"

"Never. They're astonishing."

"I've never met anyone who appreciates everything as you do. You're right, though, they are pretty cool. Did you know that you're always telling me to do that? Appreciate things, pay attention to the things around me, listen to what my senses are telling me. I've taken your advice and have been trying to do that lately. I was in the pool the other day and I shut my eyes and just focused on listening to the sounds around me. I noticed the smell of the chlorine, the sound of the bugs, the warmth of the sun. I even went down and visited the horses yesterday and I haven't gone near those two since I was a kid."

"Wow, I'm surprised you listened to me. You're always surprising me, Austen."

"And you me, Birdie."

"You shouldn't worry so much about Liza, ya know."

"Oh yeah? Why do you say that?"

"You deserve to be treated better. You deserve to be with a girl who is proud to be with you and doesn't screw your dad."

"Thanks, Birdie, but I'm not so sure I do deserve better."

"You do, you just don't know it. Take it from a girl

who has only been loved for a brief time in her life, you're not like me. You're lovable and deserve to be loved."

"You deserve to be loved, Birdie. You're probably the most interesting person I've ever met. You deserve the world."

Lying face first in the garden behind the great castle is sensational. My pores tingle with each brush of every individual blade of grass across my skin. The coolness of dew sits in contrast against the warmth of my body. Austen is speaking. I can tell because his mouth is moving but I'm not comprehending the words. I try to contribute to the conversation, but I don't think my words are translating because Austen is cackling as I try in vain to explain to him the beauty of this earth and the magic of the lawn beneath our bodies.

The glimmering light from the fireflies circle his head, creating an angelic image. His hands are folded over his chest and the moonlight gleams, casting him in an illuminating glow.

I focus on his lips, fascinated by the movement of his mouth, "Birdie, you're too funny. I bet you won't remember a word that you have said in the last hour."

"Your lips . . . are . . . perfect . . ."

"Hahahaha, thanks, Birdie. So 're yours."

~~~

I wake, opening my eyes to see Austen sleeping beside me. The moon is gone, and the sky is lighter, the sun is getting ready to peek over the horizon. The taste of lawn in my mouth is apparent as I flip over onto my back and try in desperate horror to pull blades of grass from my mouth before Austen wakes up.

It is that time of morning when everyone else is still

sleeping, but you know you only have a brief few minutes before the world awakes so you breathe in the last bit of silence while you can. The birds are chirping, already getting on with their day. I recount what happened last night, my face down on the grass, Austen laughing. God, I must have said some stupid stuff, I am kind of glad that I do not remember much. Did I tell Austen something about his lips? Geez, I hope not.

Austen stirs, turning his head towards me, and flashes his hazel eyes. "Hey, Birdie. You were a riot last night."

"Oh, god."

"Don't worry, I will only never let you live it down and remind you of my perfect lips for the rest of your life."

"Oh, god. I'm never smoking weed again."

"Famous last words. We'd better get inside before someone thinks we're doing something naughty."

"We kind of were, right?"

"Yeah, I suppose so."

Austen and I sneak back in the house through the secret entrance in back and I am grateful to see that no one is up yet so we can slip back to our rooms unnoticed. At the base of the stairs, Austen stops.

"Later, Birdie."

"Later, Austen." Austen smiles at me—a smile I have never seen from him before, and I do not know what to make of it.

Chapter Sixteen

I should not like him. I know that. He has been mean to me, cruel even. He made my last few months of my high school career almost unbearable. He mortally wounded my pride by calling me Creeper, gross, a loser. He kicked my stuff across the floor on my first day. He looked through me, never believing I deserved to be seen by him. I know all of this. I know all of this better than you do, as I lived it. But reader, let me tell you that my heartbeat quickens when he walks into a room, my blood rushes to my face whenever he says my name, and my palms get sweaty when I am close enough to smell his Irish spring body soap. Yes, I know what soap he uses, it is the same as one of my former foster brothers, Darrell. I loved the smell so much when I was twelve, he let me use it sometimes if I would agree not to tell the foster parents about his drug dealing.

Dark story aside, what I am saying is—I know what you are thinking. He does not deserve my affection. You are right. That is why even though I like him, I choose not to do anything about it, but the wall I have built to keep love out is starting to buckle. It is exactly one week after the weed incident and Austen invited me to go with him to a party and I have said no, instead choosing to stay in talking to Malcolm about his crush, Marcus, while eating popcorn as he braids my hair.

"So, have you talked to him?" I inquire, quizzically.

"Talked to who?"

"Please, you know who."

"Marcus? No, of course not. I can't seem to get the nerve."

"You shouldn't be nervous about it. What is the worst thing that could happen? That he says he doesn't like you anymore? So what, it won't kill you."

"It might."

"Ha, you want to hear my, I-could-die-of-embarrassment, story?"

"Lay it on me, girl." I dive into my pot filled adventure and Malcolm laughs so hard tears stream down his face.

"So let me get this straight, you ran into Austen in the middle of the night, you smoked weed together, you said crazy things to him, told him you love his lips, and then slept together in the garden?"

"We did not SLEEP together Malcolm, we simply slept NEAR each other."

"Okay sure, sure, so now he has texted you to go to a party with him, essentially asked you on a date, and you said no so that you can eat popcorn with your platonic gay friend?"

"Correct."

"I think he's really into you, Birdie."

"Why'd you say that? He's never liked me; he's made a point to never like me. Did I tell you he used to call me Creeper in high school?"

"Only a million times. Guys aren't that complicated, Birdie. I know you do not have a lot of experience in this department but trust me when I say he likes you. A lot. It's like a boy on the playground pulling your braid or throwing something at you. They do that when they like you and want your attention."

"That is crazy, Malcolm. And, well, too bad for him. He shouldn't have humiliated me in high school then."

"Fair point. This is kind of the best revenge. Except it would be better if you didn't like him back."

"What do you mean?"

"You are only hurting yourself by not seeing what this could be. You're denying yourself something you want because why? Did he hurt your pride? He is a stupid teenage rich boy, of course, he's an ass. That doesn't mean he's all bad. Hell, maybe he even feels bad about that."

"I doubt it. I don't think he feels at all."

"Sure, he does, he is a sad boy. I mean think about his life, his dad sleeping with his girl, and all that. Getting the last housekeeper pregnant. All right under his mother's nose. Sucks."

"I know, I thought of that already. But that doesn't mean it is okay to be mean to me."

"I know." Malcolm puts the tie in at the bottom of my beautifully manicured French braid.

"Has he ever said anything nice to you? Like, at all?

I pause before responding, nervous about Malcolm's response, "Well, he did tell me once that I was beautiful and he was pretty nice to me when we were high, although I could've imagined that entire conversation."

Malcolm's jaw drops, "Are you kidding me? He told you you're beautiful? Oh my god, Birdie, he's nuts over you."

I roll my eyes, "He just wanted sex or something. Forget it, he didn't mean it. Enough about him. Have you talked to your parents yet?"

"No way. I've decided to use you as my beard for the rest of this summer then go to college and live my life. I don't want to upset them. They will find out eventually."

"Sounds healthy."

"Shut up." We both laugh.

"Listen, I better head home. Maybe text lover boy later and see if he will stop by for a visit."

"MALCOLM."

"Come on, you know you thought it." Crap, I did too.

~~~

I resist Malcolm's suggestion and my own urges and crawl into bed at midnight without a single text to Austen. The strength to manage this accomplishment is embarrassing but I am proud of myself. I will not be one of these girls who fall all over Austen Markey. I will be better than them. I will conquer this minor attraction I have for him.

As I lay congratulating myself, my phone buzzes. *Oh no.*

WHY DID YOU NOT WANT TO COME WITH ME?

I am not sure why Austen typed this in all CAPS like he is screaming at me, but I digress. I ignore the urge to text him back and put the phone back on the nightstand, leaving his screaming text unanswered.

Buzz.

Crap.

I THOUGHT YOU LIKED MY LIPS

Crap again.

I give in and type back:

IT IS LATE AND I'M ASLEEP.

CAN I COME BY?

NO.

ILL BE THERE IN 2 MINS.

Apparently, 'no' did not register. Maybe he is bluffing and after five minutes I start to believe that, until I hear a thumping on my door.

I pull back the covers and get to the door too quickly, my desire to be elusive is dissipating.

"What do you want, Austen? I was trying to sleep." Austen is wearing a black t-shirt with his silver necklace that I have noticed before, except it is not tucked into his shirt. I am not quite sure, but I think the necklace has a turtle on the end of it. A turtle? How random. He does not seem like the nature-loving type.

"I want to know why you didn't come. And don't tell me it was to hang with Malcolm."

I sigh. "Because I can't go to parties with you."

"Why not?"

"Enemies, remember?"

"I didn't think we were enemies anymore. You said you downgraded me to a former enemy."

"I know, but that doesn't mean I'm over everything that you did to me. You can't call a girl gross and creepy and think she is just suddenly not going to be mad at you anymore just because you kissed a couple of times and got high together. Those types of insults run deep."

Austen nods and says, "Oh, yeah that makes sense. Listen Birdie, I'm sorry about that. I don't think those things about you. I wish you'd forgive me. I think you're cool and we should be friends."

Friends?

"You want to be my friend? I'm shocked."

"Yeah. Can we start over? Maybe be friends, with some benefits?" Austen is a little drunk. I can tell by the slight slur in his speech. He is vulnerable and I am too nice to be cruel to someone in his state.

"Okay, Austen. We can start over. Thank you for apologizing, but we can only be friends. Nothing more, okay?"

"Okay. Why though? I mean, why don't you want more? Most girls do."

"I'm not most girls, Austen."

"I know you're not."

"Plus, remember that I never want to fall in love. It just leads to pain. I meant it and I intend to keep it."

"Hm, you are so dark, Birdie, but fair enough. Okay, friends it is."

"Friends." We shake on it.

"Hey, I've been upgraded."

"Oh my god."

"Can I come in?"

"Fine."

Austen walks in, his body soap and beer smell following him as I make a promise to myself that I will not kiss this boy. I recite this mantra several times but as he climbs into my bed and takes off his shirt, I can feel my strength begin to drain.

Chapter Seventeen

I have twinkle lights hanging along the wall by my bed. They are dark purple. It is the girliest thing in the world, I know, but I love them. They create a sense of magic in this small room in the dungeon of this castle. I stole them off one of my many foster sisters when I fled the last foster home before coming to the castle. Her name is Blanca and she kept them under her bed so I did not think she would notice. I do not steal things normally, but I was desperate for these darn twinkle lights.

The slight purple hue creates an ambiance that is more romantic than I realized before. Tonight, is the first time I have had them on when anyone else was in my room except for Malcolm and it dawns on me that they may not be helping my *do not kiss this boy* vibe I am needing right now. Maybe I should unplug them.

Austen plays music on his phone softly as he tells me about the party, "Liza and Aiesha were there. Liza ignored me as usual, so I finally just left. It was boring anyway. I get tired of hanging out with the same people all the time. I can't wait to start school next month."

"Me, too. It's a dream I have worked hard for."

"Where are you going?" Oh shit.

"Well actually, I'm going to Alfred."

"What? You're going to the same school as me and you never said anything?"

"I didn't want you to ruin it for me."

"Ha. Wow. That's crazy. Small world, I guess. That's cool though, we can keep being friends there, too."

I hadn't reckoned on this.

"Maybe. But I will be busy becoming the person I was always meant to be, so I might not have time for boys from my previous life."

"Oh shoot, you have some high expectations for this,

don't you? Why Alfred?"

"My parents and I drove through there on a road trip once and we loved it. It's one of my last memories of them."

"Wow, I feel like a real ass. I didn't even want to go there but my mother insists."

"I think it'll be wonderful."

"I hope you're right, Birdie. You deserve it."

A couple of quiet minutes later and Austen looks to his phone, suddenly remembering something, "Hey, did you find out if you could use your phone plan on the iPhone I gave you?"

"Yeah, it's good to go." I pull out my fancy new phone, "See? I don't really know how to use it though."

"No worries, I can show you. I wasn't sure when I texted you if you still had the same phone number or not. Let me see it."

"Why?"

"I'm going to set up the playlist I created for you on here."

"Oh, okay. You put a playlist together for me?"

"It's not a big deal. Only took like two minutes."

Austen sets up the playlist then explains the song choices to me, "I know a lot of great music, but I picked things that I thought you might like. There are a few from Jessie Ware, Taylor Swift, Kygo, Lord Huron, Ed Sheeran, Blood Orange, and of course, I put a couple of my favorite Nirvana songs on here, too."

"Can we listen to one?"

"Sure."

Austen hits play on a song called *Heart-Shaped Box* and it is nothing like I imagined, but I love it immediately.

"Oh, I'm glad I wear their shirt, this song is great."

A couple of song plays later, and the soft hum of

Taylor Swift's *Lover* plays in the background as we lay in my bed silently, the purple twinkle lights casting an aura of enchantment.

The moment is spellbinding, and I sense the Universe is trying to tell me something. I resist the urge to run my finger over Austen's lips, but it is no matter as he takes the lead.

Austen turns over on his side and places his hand on my cheek, pulling my face close to his.

"I know you said you just wanted to be friends, Birdie, but all I want to do is kiss you."

I nod in agreement, too weak to do anything else and for the first time in my life, I understand why they say love can make you weak in the knees. Austen puts his lips to mine and a part of me dies. The part of me that is determined to seek revenge on Austen, to keep him at a distance, the part of me that has held off on moments that feel like this. In its place is something else, something vulnerable and scared.

~~~

That night changes us. It changes our relationship indefinitely. We spend hours kissing and touching, then fall asleep wrapped in each other's arms. We wake up the next morning and know that we can never go back to being just friends. I do not know what is happening, but I sense that it is out of my control, I am on a journey, and I cannot see how it ends yet.

It is now the end of July and in just three weeks, I will be moving into my dorm at Alfred. Knowing that Austen will be there too makes this time with him more real somehow. Knowing that we can be together is frightening and exciting at the same time. We never say we are together. We just are. The next few nights, Austen is in my room and unlike my evenings with Malcolm, he is not hesitant to touch me. I manage to keep my virginity intact but explore my sexuality slowly, with Austen's guiding hand.

Austen works hard to make up for his previous indiscretions. He compliments me and is sweet to me. I can tell that he feels bad for the way he treated me in high school. We talk a lot when we are together these few nights, I even open up to him about some of my more difficult experiences. My life is not something he can relate to, but he listens intently, trying to understand.

"So, you just get placed in different homes over and over again? Why can't you just stay in one home?"

"It is mostly due to the wants and needs of foster parents. Once a foster kid hits a certain age, most foster parents think they can handle it but then realize how hard it is, and before I know it, I'm at a new home. I was not super difficult like some of the other kids, but I did keep to myself. I never really spoke to the foster parents much. I would just try to stay invisible, I would stay in my room and read. After my parents died, I was always too afraid to get close to another family. It's so painful to lose people you love."

"Your life has been fascinating. I feel like such a jerk for ever being mean to you."

"Good, you should," we both laugh at this.

Austen brings up a brilliant idea, "Why don't we take a trip to Alfred?"

"Really? Why? We will be there soon enough."

"I know, but I want to see it before everyone else is there. I want to see it when it is quiet, see if I can decide if I'm going to like it or not. What do you think? I will drive—head there tomorrow? We can spend the day there and then drive back later that night. Plus, it'll give me a chance to do something nice for you, to make up for some of my meanness."

"Austen, you just made my day."

"Great. It's a date then."

"I would love nothing more."

"Okay, tomorrow morning, say eight a.m. let's head out. Sound good?"

"Sounds wonderful." And it truly did.

~~~

Austen went back to his room for the night, but the second he left I missed his presence so after about twenty minutes I give up and sneak out in my socks and the big white shirt he gave me to sleep in and tiptoe out of my room and up out of the dungeon.

As I near the staircase, I hear talking. My heart sinks into the soles of my feet as I recognize Liza. *No.* Are they still sleeping together? I inch close enough to hear but stay out of sight in case Liza comes down the stairs.

"What do you mean you don't want to hang out, Austen?"

"Just what I said."

"You're not even going to let me in your room?"

"No. Why don't you go find my dad?"

Liza sighs, "That whole thing ended, Austen, I'm not seeing him anymore, now I'm free to see you."

"Why would I want to see you after you've slept with my dad?"

"Because you're crazy about me."

"Not anymore. I deserve better than you."

"Are you kidding me? You're a joke. Who gave you that idea?"

"Birdie did."

"Birdie? What does she know?"

"I'm seeing her."

"WHAT?"

"You heard me, and I like her and I'm not going to let you screw this up."

"You realize she is just some poor person, right? I mean, like, she is here because she's like, homeless. She wears the same clothes all the time and I'm pretty sure she never showers."

"That's not true, she's clean and I don't care about the clothes. She doesn't have parents buying her stuff, give her a break."

"Fine, if you want to pull a girlfriend out of the dumpster, go ahead. I won't have trouble finding someone better than you."

"Good luck to him."

I flatten myself against the wall as Liza storms down the stairs and out the door, her heels clanking all the way. Tears fill my eyes, blurring my vision. I bump into the railing as I sprint my way in the dark back to my hole. I can hear Austen behind me, but I do not want him to see me cry.

"Birdie? Come back, please!"

I race downstairs and shut the door to my cave, but Austen is pushing it open before I can lock it.

"Birdie, come on, don't run from me. Please don't cry. Liza's a bitch. I am not sleeping with her, I haven't in forever. I wouldn't do that to you."

Tears are flowing freely as I stare up at this beautiful man in front of me, my insecurities on full display, "Austen, she's right. I'm nobody. We're so different. You can't be with me. I'm the help."

"Birdie, I like you. I don't care about that with you. Please, don't be upset. Will you still come with me tomorrow to Alfred? It'll be fun, I promise."

Austen's arms are wrapped around me in a bear hug, I can hear his heart beating.

"Okay."

I spend the night wrapped in Austen's arms, Liza's words taunting me in my dreams.

Chapter Eighteen

Driving through the Catskill Mountains on a perfect summer morning is captivating beyond words. As the trees whip by, the warm summer air breezing through my hair, I wish I were a professional photographer or a poet so that I may have a chance of capturing the beauty of the moment.

Austen's hair flops in the wind, his terrible voice singing along to some famous band I have never heard of, and a feeling of peace washes over me for the first time since my parents died. It's contentment; a sensation of being home. Dread inevitably follows these pleasurable feelings as I know this cannot last. Nothing good does.

"Your voice is terrible!" I yell above the noise. Austen smiles a big, toothy smile and for the first time, I notice he has a dimple on the right side. He really is lovely.

~~~

Alfred sits in a tiny bubble, a village nestled in a valley amongst the Allegheny Mountains filled with college students during the school year and townies during the summer. The small village has one main street with one stoplight. The street separates the two colleges in the town, Alfred University and Alfred College. Rivals, I am sure. They almost have to be.

Alfred's motto is *Outside of Ordinary*—and I have to agree. As we walk through the campus, I get the impression that this place is anything but ordinary. I have never seen anywhere so beautiful. Trees are lining the streets and the leaves are rustling slightly in the warm mid-day breeze. The lawns are freshly mowed, the green of the grass setting a perfect scene against the clay-colored buildings. Austen and I come across a strange, small castle-like building sitting off to itself, up slightly on a hill. I already know all about the building and could not wait to see it in person. It is made up of large stones with a sculpted top mimicking a castle you would see in Europe. This sculpting is called battlements, something I learned after excess internet searches desperate to learn anything and everything about the school, including the architecture of the buildings. Battlements were designed so that archers could position themselves and shoot at incoming enemies through slits cut out of the stone wall. Of course, for the purposes of this building, they are decorative.

I explain all of this in detail to Austen, who is looking at me like I am crazy, "How do you know all of that?"

"I've researched everything there is to know about this school."

"I don't know anything about this place, I didn't know they had a building like this here. Very cool, I must admit."

"They also have an observatory up this path," I am staring at the map I brought with me, "we should walk up and check it out."

"Let's do it."

Austen seems like he is interested in all this stuff, and I am thrilled to share it with him. I want him to see why it will be so great to be here.

Memories of driving through this small village with my adoptive parents play like elevator music in the background of my mind. I wish they were here with me now. I know they would have loved this.

~~~

It is a very warm evening. The heat from the day has settled along the ground, refusing to release its grip. After spending the next four hours visiting almost every building on this campus, me rambling on about the facts of school, Austen listening intently, we have now come to the end of this perfect day. Austen walks back to his car, an expensive white Charger, and pulls out a pack I had not noticed until now.

"What's in there?"

"Food, wine, and some blankets. I thought we'd head to a spot that my mother told me about at the top of that hill. She said you can see the entire town from up there. She drew me a map. You up for it?"

"Yes, please." I smile so big it hurts my face.

The air has a thickness to it, it settles on my skin and wraps its fingers around me, keeping me cocooned and safe. I follow Austen up one of the many hillsides in Alfred, trusting him to take me to a spot that will make this hike worth it. We finally get to the top of the hill and I turn back to admire the view in front of me. You can see the entire town from up here, the green trees and grass darkening as the sun begins to set, bugs are chittering all around us.

Austen lays a small blanket down and pulls out a couple of sandwiches from his backpack, which I notice also functions as a cooler, and a bottle of pink Moscato follows. We sit in silence for a bit, eating our ham and cheeses, taking swigs of wine, the sweetness dripping down our chins.

The sun is setting behind the hills now, dipping lower into the sky, casting an orange glow off the buildings below. A little more, and it gets a bit darker, almost dark enough to see the stars when a new light pops up out of the ground at our feet.

"I was hoping they would come out tonight."

"Fireflies. Wow, there must be hundreds of them."

Austen and I sit in awe of the insects rising from the

earth, waking up, twinkling their luminescence.

"You know that's how they find a mate? That light is them communicating with each other." Maybe Austen is more of a nature guy than I gave him credit for.

Flickering lights are all around me, rising from the depths of the soil, communicating with each other, searching for love. The small pale-yellow glowing orbs glimmer in the shadow of the setting sun.

I will remember this for the rest of my life. I will remember the warm air against my skin, the hum of fluttering insect wings, the enchanting glow from fireflies, the taste of sweetness is my mouth. Mostly, though, I will remember Austen's face. The small smile as he watches the little lights flash is laced with wonderment. I will think of all this and smile. All of my pain, heartache, loneliness, and fear are surpassed by the splendor of this moment.

The sun fades away completely and the bugs calm. Austen and I lay on our backs, searching for shooting stars for what seems like forever; unwilling to depart with such a night.

"I've never seen the night sky so vividly," I say, admiringly, "I mean, you can see the stars at your place, but not like this. This is unreal."

"Yeah, it is. I think I'm going to take astronomy next year. I had no idea the stars could be like this."

"Hmm . . . magic."

"Birdie, thanks for coming up here with me."

"Thank you, Austen, for bringing me. I'll never forget it. I don't want it to end."

"It doesn't have to," Austen turns his head to mine and kisses me.

Is it time? I think to myself about how there could never be a more glorious night to lose my virginity than this. This is the kind of night that women only ever dream of or read about in books, and here I am living it.

"Austen," I push his face back slightly, "I'm ready."

"You sure, Birdie? I don't want to do anything if you aren't."

I kiss him sweetly, "Yes, Austen, I'm sure."

Before I know it, I am wrapped in him, his hand touching every inch of my body like it has some secret to reveal, peeling off items of clothing as he does. I grip his biceps, clinging on to the curves of his muscles, embracing him as I prepare myself for what is to come.

Austen's right-hand digs into the front pocket of the backpack, pulling out a square golden package. He tears the corner edge with his teeth and puts it on quickly, he has done this a few times before. This realization starts to create anxiety in my stomach, knowing I will not live up to his previous experiences.

"I'm not going to be very good at this, Austen," I say in a low whisper.

"You don't have to worry about that, Birdie, just be you and relax. Trust me, this'll be amazing for me, it already is."

Before he enters me, he appears nervous, "What is it?" I ask.

"This might hurt so if you need to stop, just say so."

"Okay."

Austen finds me, filling me slowly, holding back restraint so that he does not hurt me. I notice a pinching sensation and then a sting, but it fades quickly as Austen starts to move in and out. I grip him as his turtle necklace hangs above me, swinging as he moves.

"You okay?"

I nod my head, "Yes, don't stop."

"Birdie. I. Think. I. Love. You."

I gasp and grip his shoulders tightly.

At that moment, I understand. The world unveils itself

to me, revealing the stuff stars and glowing orbs are made of. *Magic.*

Chapter Nineteen

I wish I could tell you that this was the moment I let it all go and embraced love. I would like to tell you that all my fear, abandonment issues, and insecurities just melted away never to rear their ugly heads again. I would like to tell you that, but it is not realistic, dear reader, as our demons like to haunt us and show their nasty selves when we are at our most vulnerable.

I can hear a buzzing. I open my eyes and glance at the world around me. The blue sky filled with morning light, our clothes scattered in the grass, the small blanket barely covering our naked bodies. My chest tightens immediately, fear clenching its tight grip on my heart. I bolt upright and grab my clothes as quickly as I can. The profound need to run away from this moment, from these feelings slaps me across the face.

Austen stirs and wakens, startled by my rapid movements, "Birdie, what's wrong?"

He is rubbing his eyes and looking very confused as I slip my shoes on, "I have to go."

"Where? I'll get us home, don't worry."

"NO. No, Austen, that's your home, not mine. I don't have a home. Liza was right I'm homeless."

"What's going on, Birdie? Why are you freaking out right now?"

"Please, just get dressed and let's go. I don't want to be here anymore."

~~~

The ride home in the car is painfully quiet but the voice in my head is screaming. Here I am, in love with this guy and I know better. He does not want me. He will just leave me like everyone does. How am I going to date some rich kid? How would that even work? Why did I do this to myself? Why have I made life so hard by complicating it with love?

We finally pull up to the castle and I open the door and race inside before the car has even come to a complete stop.

I can hear Austen in the distance, "Birdie, wait!"

~~~

The final days at the castle are awkward. Austen texts me several times but I leave them unread. I only come out of the safety of my room to complete my job duties. I avoid all social interactions and go to great lengths to do so, once hiding in the cleaning closet under the stairs when I heard footsteps.

Liza and Aiesha knock on my bedroom door several times, each time I ignore them. Malcolm calls me twice and I hit silent.

I just need to get to Alfred. I need to flee this place.

~~~

Finally, move-in day has arrived. My dreams are coming true. I hop on a train to take me on the journey to college, trying desperately to be as excited for this moment as I should be, but the excitement is tainted. It's as though black ink has been poured all over my masterpiece and no matter how much I try to scrub it away, a dark tint lingers over my heart.

The world whips by in a haze as I stare out the smudgy window, reminding me of the drive up here with Austen. I wish I had not blown up my relationship with him, I wish I were stronger. As a kid who grew up without her parents and bounced around from home to home, I have some of the classic foster kid characteristics: skittish, nervous, untrusting, paranoid, jaded, but mostly I am afraid. It's something that I accept, the fear. I am afraid of heartbreak, afraid of not being good enough, afraid of rejection.

I guess this is as good of a time as any to read Austen's texts. I consider deleting them completely but am unable to. I take a deep breath and click on the envelope by his name and start at the beginning.

Birdie, please talk to me, it's been days

I'm so sorry

We shouldn't have slept together, you werent ready, forgive me

I'm so worried about u, can u at least text me back so I know ur ok

The most painful texts are the last two:

I should not have told u that I love u

I will leave u alone at Alfred

In a desperate attempt to avoid heartbreak, I end up breaking my heart and his. The irony is not lost on me. What have I done? How could I do this to him?

Chapter Twenty

My spirits lift a little when I finally arrive in Alfred. I will try to appreciate this for all that it is. I shake my head hoping the sadness will drain from my ears and race up to the dorm room I have been assigned with my trash bag of belongings hoping nobody sees me with the bag.

The stairs creak as I make my way through the old dormitory, the one with individual rooms and co-ed floors, something that makes me feel very grown-up. The building has an old musky smell to it, and I inhale deeply, solidifying the memory in my head forever. My room is tiny, room 316. It's just big enough for a single bed, dresser, and closet. It has a big window, though, that looks out to the rolling green hills in back. There is a pathway at the top of the hill with students walking, the cloud speckled blue sky as their backdrop.

The room is simple, but it's mine. I dump my belongings onto the bed, and it occurs to me that as I stand in this barren room with the few things I own, that I do not have all that I am going to need, such as sheets or a comforter. I will have to wrap myself in the one blanket I bought for six dollars from a thrift store last year and a pillow I have been taking with me ever since my third foster home. My entire life is laid out before me and it's pathetic: one blanket, one stolen pillow, a stolen set of purple twinkle lights, a beat-up copy of *Pride and Prejudice*, one Ariel doll, three pairs of jeans, six pairs of underwear, five t-shirts, one hoodie, three pairs of socks, a toothbrush and toothpaste, a box of tampons, and a few hair ties.

With the little bit of money I have saved up, I will buy a couple of new shirts, some sheets, shampoo and conditioner, and maybe some grown-up makeup like lipstick and mascara. I start my federal work-study job in the alumni building next week so that will help.

After I hang my purple lights and tuck my few clothes into the dresser, I take a walk around the building. Other students are moving in and unpacking, but it is taking them a lot longer because they have way more stuff than me. TVs, microwaves, heaters, art for their walls, lots of clothes, computers, and mini fridges. I bet they do not even appreciate half of it. I do wish I had a computer though. It's going to be tough in these modern times to not have a computer in college, but I will be able to use the computers in the library.

Now I need to work on making friends. Friendships that I want to last the rest of my life, the kind you see in movies. How do I do that? For the first time in my life, I am trying to make friends and it occurs to me that I have no idea how.

A girl with big bouncy curls opens her door just as I walk by, "Hey, I'm Abrianna, what's your name?"

Yes. She wants to talk to ME. "Birdie, you a first-year too?"

"Yup, sure am, my parents just left to head back to Pennsylvania. Where are you from?"

"New York City."

"So cool, do you have your room set up yet?"

"Yup. You?"

"It's gonna to take me forever to get everything put away and my posters hung. I want to head down and get some food. You wanna come?"

"Love to."

Maybe it is not so hard to make friends after all.

Chapter Twenty-One

Abrianna and I become fast friends. She has an interesting background, the daughter of a wealthy mixed-race family. Her mother is Jewish and her father is black and Catholic. Her personality is infectious, she is constantly optimistic and always swatting down my skepticism. We make for quite the pair. I don't know why she wants to hang out with me all of the time, but she does, plus, she is endlessly fascinated by my history. She says she wants to write a book about my life one day. We spend the first week together almost every minute. I open up to her more than I have anyone, except for maybe Malcom, I even share a lot of my secrets with her about my childhood.

"You have experienced such a unique life, Birdie. It should be documented. *From Foster Care to Alfred.* That should be the title of the book."

"My story might be unique but it's not that interesting. I don't have a ton of exciting stories to tell. My life didn't really start happening until I spent the last summer cleaning a castle."

"You cleaned a castle?"

"Not a literal castle but yeah, a big rich person's house. Big enough that they had live-in help and horses. That's not even the interesting part. In the house lived Austen, my arch nemesis. It's his family home. Austen was my bully during my last semester of high school. He called me Creeper and told me I was gross and let's just say it ended up being an interesting summer. To make matters crazier, he goes here."

"What? Let me get this straight, the rich kid whose family you worked for and you hooked up with over the summer is here in Alfred?"

"Wait, how did you guess we hooked up?"

"Oh, come on Birdie, it's soooo obvious. Did you have sex or just make out? Was it your first time?"

"Damn, you're good."

"I know. What're you gonna do if you see him here?"

"Ugh, I don't even want to think about it."

"Hmm it sounds like you need a distraction. College should be good for that. There's a party down at one of the off-campus houses on Saturday. You in?"

"Definitely!"

"I wonder if Austen will be there."

"Oh no, I hope not."

"I hope so, I'd love to meet the guy. What happened? Why did you break up?"

"I don't think we were ever really together to begin with. I kind of panicked and ghosted him the morning after we had sex and he told me he loved me, and I didn't say it back."

"WHAT? Ouch. Poor guy. All well, there will be others. Let's find you a new Austen."

I love this girl.

~~~

My first college party. I can't believe this is finally happening. I borrow Abrianna's low cut sparkly green tank top and pair it with my trusty black jeans and I must say, I look pretty darn good. Abrianna puts mascara on me, a smudge of blush, and a pink lip. She looks her usual amazing self, effortlessly rocking a fitted t-shirt showing off her chest that any girl would be envious of. Thanks to her, I think I might actually pass as cool at this party.

The house sits high up on a hill at the end of a street. It is a large, old, run-down, Victorian-style with a wrap-around front porch. I can only assume boys live here due to the state of it being a total catastrophe. Beer cans and bottles are everywhere, pizza boxes piled high and lawn chairs serve as the furniture. Abrianna and I scoot past the hordes of people to find Evan, Abrianna's crush from down the hall who invited us here, standing in the kitchen.

"There he is, the one in the blue shirt," Abrianna points. Evan is tall with broad shoulders and plays on the football team and it's easy to see why Abrianna is a fan. He reminds me a lot of Malcolm thanks to his tall, dark, and handsome presence. He smiles and I can practically hear Abrianna's heart beating in response.

Evan comes towards Abrianna the second he spots her. He is clearly as smitten as she, "Hey Abrianna, I'm glad you made it," they embrace, "you must be Birdie, it's nice to meet you."

I shake Evan's strong hands and instantly like him, "Nice to meet you, too."

"Follow me, ladies, I want you to meet the rest of the team." The team? I hope Austen isn't here, he told me he was going to try out for the football team.

Evan leads Abrianna by the hand through dozens of people who are in varying stages of drunkenness until we are outside. A group is standing around a beer pong table and it only takes me about five seconds to spot Austen. There is no escaping now as he is wide-eyed and staring at me.

"Hey guys, this is my girl Abrianna and her friend Birdie." Abrianna shoots me a look and I know we will need to talk about 'my girl' later.

"Hey" is said in unison but Austen stays silent, he is looking away from us, now clearly preparing to ignore me for the rest of the night.

Evan gestures for us to sit on a couch, yes, a couch in the backyard, that has a couple making out on one end.

Abrianna and I sit as close to each other as possible, not wanting to disturb them.

"We're playing beer pong. You two can join after this round."

Austen has inched farther away and is now standing on the other side of the table trying desperately to fade into the background.

I lean in to whisper to Abrianna, "That's him."

"Who? Austen?"

"Shh, yes. The guy in the black t-shirt on the other side of the table."

Abrianna spots him, "Oh, he's really cute. I can see why you lost it to him."

I give her my best Shut. The. Hell. Up face and she laughs, "Just kidding, I hate him." I wish I could hate him, but Austen is hard for me to hate now, which is super frustrating because I used to be so good at it.

One game of beer pong later and Evan is teaching Abrianna how to play while Austen has turned his back and is having a conversation with some brunette in a crop top. After a couple rounds of beer pong, I am well on my to being drunk for the first time in my life. The stale taste of beer is repugnant but the warm feeling in my belly is delightful. My inhibitions must be down because all I want to do is talk to Austen.

"Don't do it, Birdie. Boys that good looking are dangerous." Abrianna says in a hurried, slurry fashion.

"I can't help it. I miss him and I was so mean to him. I just want a chance to explain."

"He was mean to you first. Didn't you say he was a jerk to you in high school?"

I no longer hear her as I ease my way over in his direction, trying to look mysterious and cool but failing thanks to the slight hobble in my step.

"Hey, Birdie. You want another?" Evan asks.

"Sure, thanks, Evan."

"Have you met Austen yet? He's on the team."

"Uh, yeah."

I must have a strange look on my face because he says, "Oh. You two know each other?"

Austen does not respond but shrugs and looks at me with an unreadable expression.

"Oh, uh, I better go grab you that drink."

After Evan walks away, Austen says, "You feel okay? You seem drunk. Have you ever been drunk before?"

"No."

"Well, you'd better chill . . . later," Austen turns to walk away.

"I'm sorry, Austen."

Austen turns back, looking at me like I shot him, "It's too late for that, Birdie."

"Austen wait, I miss you." *Damn, I'm a wreck.*

Austen turns back towards me, "Really? You do? You ghosted me completely right after we slept together. I know I was mean to you in high school, but I don't think I deserved that."

"I know, but I want to explain," this comes out more slurred than I wanted.

Austen cold expression stabs me in the heart. "I don't care about your explanation."

~~~

My purple lights are casting a moody hue over the shattered pieces of me. I use my blanket to wipe my eyes as I replay every song on the playlist Austen made me over and over again. The lyrics *I've been locked inside your heart-shaped box for weeks* just hits different now that my heart is broken.

Chapter Twenty-Two

Abrianna is desperate to cheer me up. My heart is aching, though, and so I don't know if I'll ever recover, despite her efforts.

"Birdie, we've got to get you out of this funk. He's just a boy."

"I know, but it's more than that, though. I'm crazy over him and I pushed him away. I'm so afraid to open up to someone, I used to think that was a good thing. I used to believe that I'd be able to open up when I was out of the system and ready to have real relationships in my life, but I guess not."

"Birdie, we're all afraid of love. It's so scary. Rejection is the worst. But despite how it feels right now, I promise you that it won't kill you."

"It was just so embarrassing. I know people saw and heard what he said, what I said. Maybe I should transfer to another school."

Adrianna rolls her eyes, "You're sooo dramatic. No one heard, they were all too drunk to remember even if they did."

"I wish I hadn't pushed him away. I wish I weren't so afraid. I thought I was stronger than I am."

"Look, I'm no expert but considering your past, I mean, it's no wonder you're afraid to get close to people."

"I don't know what to do about it, Abrianna, I want to get over this."

"I know. Okay, so don't be offended but I talked to my mom about you."

"What? She must think I'm pathetic. Well, her and everyone else at that party."

"Not at all, she is a shrink so hear me out. She said your fear of abandonment is heavily influencing your life.

She said it might be good for you to try to find out about your story. I mean, who the hell left you at a train station and why? It would torture me not to know."

"I have a fear of abandonment?"

"Maybe, I dunno. It's just what she said."

"So, she thinks that I should find out about my past?"

"My mom is always saying that people need to dive headfirst into their issues so that they can resolve them. Maybe she is right, Birdie."

"Hmm," the image of the letter tucked into the back of *Pride and Prejudice* flashes into my mind's eye, "I do have a hint about who I came from."

"A hint?"

"Yeah, I got a letter when I was sixteen from the adoption agency. Apparently, some guy was trying to reach out to me because he thought he might be my birth father."

"What? That's crazy, did you call him? What happened?"

"Nothing, I folded it up and put it in a book."

"Oh my gosh, aren't you curious, Birdie?"

"Yeah, I am. It's just painful. I mean, I was abandoned as a baby, I wasn't wanted. It's not something I like to think about."

"I get that, but you don't really know that you weren't wanted."

"How do you mean?"

"What if your birth mother had a reason, like she wanted you, but she couldn't take care of you. There are probably a million reasons why someone gives up a baby, but it doesn't mean they don't care about the baby."

I shrug, "I guess so."

"Do you want to find out?"

"What do you mean?"

"Where is the letter? Maybe read it again."

I consider this, then grab my book sitting on the small dresser and open the back cover, "Here it is."

Abrianna opens it up slowly, then reads: "David Johnson would like for you to contact him if you are interested. He believes he may be your birth father."

"There's a phone number and an address but the address is a church, which is weird, what do you think, Birdie? What do you want to do?"

"I don't want to call him. I don't know what I'd say."

"Should we go there?"

"Go where? New Hope?"

"Yeah, my class was cancelled today so I have the whole weekend. I don't think New Hope is that far away, I have been through there before with my family. We could take my car."

"You would do that? Come with me?"

"Sure, it'd be an adventure, plus this is a big deal, I don't think anyone should do something like this alone."

"Okay, okay. You're right. I mean, why not. I could always change my mind and we could just come back."

"Exactly. Come on, Birdie, it's early, we have all day. Let's go."

~~~~

The drive is about five hours long, so I fill in Abrianna about what I know on the way, which isn't much. All I know about my story is that I was found wrapped in a towel outside the front door of the train station in New Hope. The police were never able to figure out where I came from or who left me. They were unable to determine if someone in the town left me there or if a person riding on the train chose this spot to leave me before heading on their way. We also spend hours plotting what I would say to David Johnson if I do meet him.

"Hello, David Johnson? I am Elizabeth Wright and you tried contacting me a few years ago. I happened to be in town and thought I would stop by. Oh my god that sounds so stupid."

"No, it doesn't, I mean, it'll get the job done."

As we drive, I allow myself to think about who my mother might be. I have managed to keep thoughts of her at bay for most of my life but, today, they have risen out of the deep recesses of my mind and are sitting right on top.

What is she like? Why did she not want me? Why was I unlovable? I curl up in my seat, hoping that Abrianna does not see the tears streaming down my face as I press myself against the window, watching the world streak by in a flurry of color.

~~~

I must have dozed off. My neck kinks in pain as I lift my head off the window. I rub it and check the time on my phone.

"Oh my god, Abrianna, you shouldn't have let me sleep!"

"It's cool girl. I thought you might need some rest before we do this. If you change your mind, let me know and we will head right back."

"Where are we going to stay tonight? I haven't started work yet so I don't have any money."

"No worries, I have money for a room."

"I'll pay you back."

"Don't worry about it, instead let me use this trip in a book I'm going to write about you one day."

"Ha, okay," I say, not really believing her.

"I think we're close."

We are one exist from New Hope and my heart feels like it might burst through my chest. What do I hope to find here?

Abrianna slows the car down as we near the exit, but my heart rate speeds up.

We pull into what appears to be, a very small town and are immediately on what we presume is the main street of New Hope. Little cute shops line the streets and without even trying, we spot a strange looking building and realize it's the train station. It's small, but a much cuter building than I ever expected a train station to be. The best word to describe it is whimsical. There is a small tower-like structure on one end, reminding me of Hogwarts or a witch's house in a fairytale.

Abrianna pulls the car into a parking spot at the station, "Wow, that was easy. I do kind of remember this town being very small though. But I don't remember this train station. What a cool building. Would this have been where you were left?"

I nod, "Yeah, I guess so."

"Want to get out and check it out?"

"Sure," I hesitate, "we are here, so might as well."

We walk up the sidewalk toward the station and there are indications that the railroad and building are important to the town everywhere. Several signs are posted about the "Historic Railroad" and guided tours. So, I was left at a tourist spot? Why? To be sure I was seen? The heaviness at being in this place, knowing that I was left here sometime eighteen years ago, sits on my lungs, making it hard for me to breathe. I need to be somewhere else.

"Let's walk around the town."

"Okay, Birdie. You okay?"

"I'm trying to be."

We leave the train station quickly, cross the street, and

head down another street towards the unknown. I glimpse around me and spot a bridge crossing a river, the Delaware River, according to the large green street sign.

I point at it, "Let's head for that bridge."

We change direction and stop at the foot of the old rusted green bridge and look around. I remind myself to breathe. I try to settle myself while absorbing the sites around me. The town is adorable, clean, and has that perfect small-town New England feel to it. I bet this would have been a lovely place to grow up, it's so different from New York City, so much calmer.

We cross the bridge as families walk by, bicycles fly by, and there is an overall feeling of cheer in the air. A small, blonde-haired child is eating a sandwich in one hand and clutching a doll in the other, reminding me of the Ariel doll my adoptive parents gave me. I wish they were here now, providing support as I go through this, but I glance over to Abrianna—I'm so grateful to have her here with me. I am not sure I could've done this alone. The sandwich the child is eating reminds me that I am starving.

"Hey, I'm starving, you?"

"Oh yeah, definitely. Let's find somewhere to eat."

After about twenty minutes of walking, we come across a small diner that is similar to the kind from the fifties that you see in movies. We pop in and sit at the counter. I have so much adrenaline running through me that my hands are shaking. Luckily, Abrianna doesn't seem to notice.

"What can I get you two?" Asks the waitress on the other side of the counter who looks to be in her thirties, attractive with a whiff of sadness to her.

"An iced tea and grilled cheese, please," I say the first thing I see on the menu, not having the mental ability to make any deeper of a decision than that.

"Same for me."

"Sure thing, say, what's your name, hun?" The sad waitress asks as she pours the tea. "Are you from here?"

"Um, no, not really. My name is Birdie. We're just in town for today."

"Oh." She looks at me quizzically. I must have said something strange.

"Well, I don't mean to stare but you remind me of someone I used to know as a teenager. It's uncanny how much you look like her. I was wondering if you were a cousin of hers or something. I know she never had kids." What? Oh no. I look like someone she knows? I have never reminded anyone of anyone else before in my life.

"Oh no, it couldn't be." Please just give me my tea and go away.

"So strange." She puts the glass in front of me and pulls out a straw, "I will be back with your grilled cheeses."

Abrianna flashes me a wide-eyed look, "Shit, Birdie."

Who is this person I remind her of? Could it be someone I am related to? How can I find out without giving away my secret?

~~~

Two sandwiches and several plots later, we have selected a plan on how to ask the waitress about the person she says I resemble. She brings over the change after Abrianna pays the bill with cash. She hands it over slowly, glancing at me.

This is my chance, so I jump on the opportunity, "Hey, just out of curiosity, what is the name of the person I remind you of? Maybe I know her. I think I do have some family here."

She lifts her eyebrow at me before replying, "Well, her

name was Janet Marie. She died several years ago but we were friends in school."

"Oh, nope. I don't recognize the name."

"That's okay, but you do look like her."

With that, we shuffle out the door before she can ask any more questions.

~~~

Outside the diner, I sit on a nearby bench as the world spins around me. Abrianna is on her phone searching the name Janet Marie, New Hope, PA.

"All that comes up is an obituary. It says: Janet Marie, born May 1st, 1986, died tragically on Sunday, June third, 2013, at the age of twenty-seven. Janet Marie leaves behind a mother, Dorothea Marie, and her extended church family at St. John Evangelist Roman Catholic Church. She was loved greatly by those who knew her and followed the word of God with an open heart. Information about services to follow."

I look up at Abrianna, and she knows instantly, "Hey, is that the name of the church in your letter?"

"Possibly."

"Do you think that could be a coincidence?"

I shrug, "There's something else, Abrianna. Janet Marie died on my thirteenth birthday."

"WHAT? Birdie, there's no way. This is huge. I feel like Nancy Drew right now."

Who was this person? How did she die? Do I look like her? We can't find a single picture of on the internet. Disheartened, we move on to the next clue. I pull the small backpack off my shoulder and unzip it, pushing past my wallet to find my copy of *Pride and Prejudice*. It is like a security blanket; I tend to take it everywhere with me. I grip the book tightly in my hand until I build up the nerve to open to the back page.

My hand is shaking as I open the back cover and run my finger over the folded piece of, now yellowed, paper. I unfold the letter slowly. I read again quickly, reminding me of the facts as I hold my breath.

"It's definitely the same church."

"Should we go there? What do you want to do, Birdie?"

St. John Evangelist Roman Catholic Church. Another coincidence? Why is a church even listed as his address? Is he a priest or something? I thought they could not have sex? I stand up while deep in thought and begin walking, Abrianna is quick to look up directions.

"We're headed in the right direction. It's not far from here, only a couple blocks."

I am not sure of what I will find when we get there but my heartstrings are tugging me towards something, something real.

~~~

Could Janet Marie have been my mother? Surely not, the chances of me walking into New Hope and the only person I have spoken to connecting me to my mother is small. As we walk down Bridge Street towards the church, my hope of discovering something about who I am begins to grow inside me. Hope is dangerous to have when you're a foster child, some of us spend years hoping for a family to love them only to never get one. Hope is powerful, though, because once it begins to rise from the depths of your soul, it continues to do so, until it gets to the surface and threatens to be unleashed.

The church dominates the block. It's steep and pointy pinnacles looming overhead. I have been inside a church only a few times in my entire life when I stayed for six months at a super religious foster home. I was dragged to their Baptist church on Sundays while I fought tooth and nail. I have no interest in church. After my adoptive parents died, I have been hard-pressed to believe in any kind of God.

I push open the door and find the inside empty, a few candles lit at the front, casting a warm glow over the gray floors. Light is streaming in through the stained-glass windows reminding me of the castle and Austen. Abrianna puts a supportive hand on my shoulder, encouraging me to go inside. We pick a pew near the front, I sit down slowly, feeling lost but somehow also found. I am so nervous to meet David Johnson. It is going to be so awkward to say, "Hello, sorry it has been three years since you reached out, but I am the girl you believe to be your daughter," I might give the poor guy a stroke.

Heavy footsteps are walking behind us. I turn slightly and see someone coming up the aisle. As the person nears, I can see that it is a very elderly woman who is slightly hunched over as she shuffles her way to me.

"Hello."

"Hello."

"I'm Adelaide. Are you just here to pray my dears or did you need to speak to Father Johnson?"

Father Johnson? So, he is the priest.

"Uh, yeah, I do need to speak with Father Johnson. Is he around?"

"He just left to run an errand, but he should be back shortly if you want to wait."

"Um, okay, sure. We'll wait."

"Okay, I'll let you know when he comes back." The woman turns and inches her way back down the aisle.

"You sure about this, Birdie?" Abrianna's usual optimistic self seems to be waning a bit as her concern for me grows.

My nervous energy builds as I contemplate how I even got here to begin with, "We came all this way, seems like the universe wants me here."

"Ladies?" The elderly woman startles us.

"He's back in his office if you want to follow me."

"Okay, he doesn't mind us interrupting him, does he?"

"Not at all, dear." We follow behind, her body moves at a painful rate, I can practically hear her bones creaking.

Abrianna whispers, "Do you want me to go in with you?" I nod. *Please.*

"Right in here," she points into a room to her right.

"Thanks, Adelaide," I hear a man's voice say.

I peek around the corner of the room to see a man sitting behind a desk, a cross hanging above him. He appears to be very young for a priest, I always picture them as really old men, but he might be only in his thirties or so. He must be new or something. He has a warm face, and he has a concerned brow.

"Hello."

"Hi, Father Johnson," I say as Abrianna and I both enter the room.

"What can I help you ladies with today?"

I look to Abrianna, suddenly unable to speak, she takes the hint, "Hello, Father Johnson. My name is Abrianna, um, is your name David?"

"Why, yes, it is. Why do you want to know?"

Abrianna looks to me for the go ahead, I nod, "Well, this is Elizabeth Wright." David's folded hands instantly clench and his back straightens.

The young priest's mouth parts and his eyes widen, shock is evident. "Elizabeth Wright? Um, are you the same Elizabeth Wright that I reached out to several years ago?"

Now it is time for me to word vomit, "I'm sorry to come here without contacting you first and so long after you reached out. I'm not trying to freak you out. Coming here was not planned, we just left college, Alfred University, and drove here today."

The priest looks at me intently, as though he is trying to solve some sort of problem, "Woah, woah, it's okay, Elizabeth. I'm just a bit shocked. Please take a seat."

I grab the chair in front of me and sit down, my hands are tremble as I grip the straps on my backpack.

"I'm sorry it took me so long to contact you, Elizabeth. The agency would not give me your direct address, but they said they would contact you on my behalf, but when I never heard back, I wondered if they ever actually did or not."

"They did, I got a letter from them with your name, phone number, and address when I was sixteen, but I was not ready to handle the information."

"I understand. I'm glad you are here now."

"I'm going to wait in the hall. Call for me if you need me, Birdie." I watch as Abrianna steps into the hallway.

"How much do you know about where you came from, Elizabeth?"

"Not much really, just that I was abandoned as a baby at the train station. I'm just here, searching for, I don't know, the truth I guess."

"How old are you now, eighteen?"

"Yes, I just turned eighteen on June third."

"Hm. Well, thanks for coming here. I was so hoping to hear from you someday. I have a lot to explain. Would you and your friend like to stay for dinner? Are you here for the night?"

"Um, yes, we can stay for dinner. We considered getting a hotel room for the night."

"Well, come with me, my home is connected to the church, I can order delivery and we can talk. I have a spare bedroom as well if you're interested."

~~~

We are sitting in a small kitchen with bare walls. There is little to no decoration of any kind in David's home, other than a few crosses. David is quiet and I have never been more nervous in my life. I wonder if he is as nervous as I am. I doubt that is even possible.

A few moments after we finish eating Chinese food, the young priest brings out a couple of photographs. He sits next to me, appearing edgy, as he says, "This is Jane." A woman peers back at me with dark eyes and even darker hair, her face just like mine but prettier.

"Do you mean Janet Marie?" I am so glad that Abrianna is not afraid to ask questions.

"Yes, how do you know her name?"

"We were at a diner before we came to see you and the waitress said that I looked like a girl she was friends with as a teenager, and I asked about her. We looked up the name and found an obituary but nothing else. How did you know her?"

"Oh, I see, that was Stephanie. Jane and Stephanie were good friends when they were in high school. I knew Jane most of her life."

He hesitates before continuing, "She grew up in this church with me. My uncle was the priest when we were kids here. My father had me out of wedlock with a woman who didn't want me, and he wasn't in a place to take care of a child, so he left me with his brother when I was ten. My uncle wasn't able to adopt me formally, priests can't adopt children because they give their lives to God, but he allowed me to live in the guest room here under the condition—that I would learn from him and eventually attend a seminary so that one day, I could join the priesthood and take over the church after he died. He wanted this place to continue under his vision and saw me as an opportunity to ensure that happened. Jane and I were friends for years, she was in the choir and I loved to watch her sing. We wanted to be more than friends, but my uncle would not allow me to date, he wanted me to focus on God, not girls. Jane was lovely, though, I cared for her deeply."

"What happened to her?" Thanks again Abrianna.

David is rubbing the back of his head now, his hand holding the photograph is shaking as he looks at Jane, "She died in 2013 of suicide. The truth is, we were all shocked. It was so unlike her. She was very religious. No one knows why she did it, but I have my suspicions."

"The date she died, it's my thirteenth birthday."

"I know, that is actually what confirmed my suspicions."

"What were your suspicions?"

"Well, back about eighteen years ago, on June third, as you know, a newborn baby was left at the train station here in New Hope. No one ever knew who left her there. The entire town became wrapped up in who the baby was and where she came from. Everyone cared about her immensely, they nicknamed her Baby Hope," he pauses while I try to remind myself to breathe, "I suspected, but never said to anyone, that it was Jane's baby. She had been acting strangely for a few months prior and about eight or nine months before Baby Hope was left at the train station, Jane and I had sex. It was both our first time and my only time. It was a profound moment of weakness for myself, and I should regret it, but I don't. It must have been part of God's plan. However, I was devastated because Jane never spoke to me again. She would come to church and just pretend like she didn't see me. I long worried that the baby was mine. Jane and I were so young, only fifteen. My uncle would have killed me, or worse, kicked me to the streets, and her mother,

Dorothea, is a mean woman. She would never have tolerated such a thing. Seeing you now, how much you look like Jane, I can't believe it."

My mouth drops, "Why didn't you ask her about it?" My voice is rising.

"I am not proud of it, Elizabeth,"

"Birdie, please," I say correcting him.

"I am not proud of it, Birdie. The truth is . . . I was terrified of my uncle and when I was young, I didn't want to end up without a home. I had nowhere else to turn. Even after I became an adult, I was still afraid of him, of what he would think and say about it. He died three years ago and contacting the adoption agency was the first thing that I did, after I buried him. The worry has been sitting on my chest for a long time and I needed to solve the mystery. I should have reached out sooner. I shouldn't have let my fear of him stop me from doing the right thing. I should have put my trust in God."

"You sound pretty confident that you believe you and Jane are my biological parents."

"I believe so, but we would need science to prove it. But yes, especially seeing you now. You remind me so much of her. You have her face shape and eyes. You are just as beautiful as she was."

My entire body is shaking, "I can't believe I'm here talking to you. I never imagined that I would meet you honestly. I got that letter from the adoption agency and I tucked it away, it was too hard for me to deal with at sixteen. Not that I am much better prepared now."

"God works in mysterious ways and he wouldn't have wanted you here unless it was for a good reason. Listen, stay here for the night. Please, I have a guest room. I have more photographs of Jane, and we can talk more if you are okay with that?" David looks nervous as he blinks his brown eyes.

"Okay, thanks, David. Abrianna, is that okay with you?" Abrianna is quiet but nods.

David smiles but he seems to be teetering on the edge of tears. I am not sure how I feel about potentially being the daughter of a priest who cries. It is not looking like we have much in common.

~~~

"Janet Marie was a beautiful woman. She was quiet, reserved, smart with a clever sense of humor. We loved each other but after what we did, the sin we committed, I understand why she wouldn't speak to me anymore. She knew we could never do it again. I've never been with another woman since, I remember Jane having several relationships, but I know she never married."

I learn all kinds of things about who I suspect was my birth mother, "She hated peanut butter but loved chocolate. So, when we were young, she would steal the candies out of my uncle's candy jar in his office and he always had peanut butter cups. She would lick the chocolate off and throw away the peanut butter. I always thought that was so funny, I would tease her about it all the time." I also hate peanut butter but love chocolate. I tuck this information into a corner in my heart.

"She loved old black and white movies. She would talk about them all the time. And I remember her favorite flower was a sunflower. She had a dress with sunflowers printed on it and she wore it all the time. She wanted nothing more than to be a good daughter to her mother who raised her on her own after her father ran off. Jane believed that her mother was deeply ashamed of being divorced and she blamed Jane for her husband running off with another woman. Jane was just a baby when her father left and Dorothea had said once that if she had never had a baby, her husband would never have left her. Jane never met her father and only knew that he had a new wife and lived in Phoenix. I don't know his name, or I'd tell you."

"How was Dorothea mean to her? Do you know?"

"Dorothea was always telling her what a disappointment she was, she ran a very strict household. I don't think she physically abused Jane but did a number on her verbally. Jane used to share these problems with me at church. I think she told me because she knew that I could relate—because of how strict my uncle was, although he was not cruel to me, just really strict. I thought I knew her well, better than anybody, but apparently not because I was shocked when she took her own life." I can tell David holds a lot of guilt around Jane's suicide. He looks like the wind was knocked out of his chest when he mentions it.

"Did she leave a note or anything?" Abrianna asks as she sips the tea David made us.

"Well, according to Dorothea, she did. She said that it just read: 'Mother, forgive me' but no one else ever saw the note so I don't know."

I must look as exhausted as I feel because David says, "Listen, this has been a big day for us both. Why don't we get some sleep? I will give you the address of where Jane is buried in case you want to visit her tomorrow, plus, here, you can have this photo of her since you liked it so much." In the picture she is smiling, sitting in the grass under a tree, holding a book. I just wish I could see what book it was so I could read it, too.

~~~

I crawl into the small guest bed next to Abrianna who falls asleep within seconds. Her light snoring is comforting but I am still too anxious to sleep. The night is quiet and calm, but my head and heart are anything but. I throw the thin blanket off me. I need to get some air.

At night, the occasional train horn is the only sound that cuts through the silence of New Hope. Even the river seems to go still after dark. The church is imposing—it stares down at me as I sneak out of David's house. A small cemetery is in the back, so I make my way to it, ignoring the judgement from the church as I do.

I am careful not to step directly on the graves, weaving between them instead. It's nine p.m. but it feels much later with the entire town already asleep. I sit underneath the only tree in the cemetery, a large weeping willow, its long limbs reaching down to comfort me.

A glimmer catches my eye, a bit in the distance. I strain my eyes to search for the source, there it is again, a tiny flicker.

Fireflies.

Not many, just a few are still awake, hovering between the gravestones. Are they speaking to each other or to me? I watch intently, trying to decipher what they are trying to tell me.

The glow from their bodies begins to torment me. Their flashing becomes rapid, their wings fluttering so loudly they pierce my ears. I can see Janet Marie sitting in the grass, leaning back against a headstone, looking at me with pain in her eyes, fireflies lighting up all around her.

I race back to the house to escape.

I jump into the guest bed and pull the cover over my head, panting and weeping quietly trying not to disturb Abrianna. I should not have come here.

Chapter Twenty-Three

David makes us breakfast before he goes to church. He is a simple, kind man, one that I am okay with calling my father although he seems kind of boring, but then again how interesting can you be if you are a priest? We agree to have our DNA tested and he will be in touch with me with the arrangements.

I turn back to see the young priest waving. He looks serious as he stands in his garb with the church as the backdrop. The sun is low as we hike back down towards the bridge where Jane jumped. It is unnerving to walk in her steps. I run my hand across the metal of the bridge, scraping my fingernails over the ridges. The cool metal reverberates in my chest, vibrating the loose strings tying the pieces of my broken heart together.

~~~

We make the short journey to the little cemetery where Janet Marie lives. It's on a lonely edge of town, tucked behind a parking lot. It takes a while, but we finally locate her grave hidden in a corner part of the lot. There is not a single flower or memento left on her grave. Her epitaph is brief: Here lies Janet Marie, daughter, and friend.

I pick some wildflowers in a field nearby and lay them across the stone. A deep, dark part of me always hoped that one day I would get to meet her, but not like this.

The sun has now shifted to mid-sky and we begin our journey back to the car. I am silent. Overwhelming loneliness carves out my insides, leaving an empty space in my chest. My heart remains but its shattered pieces crumble. Why did I need to know all of this? What was the point?

Abrianna tries to bring me back from the edge, "Hey, girl. How you doin'? This has been a crazy trip. I hope you're happy we came here."

"I don't know how I feel. I'm kinda feeling everything, ya know?" Abrianna smiles and wraps her arm around my shoulder.

The heels of my black boots tap along the cement as we make our way back to the car, walking past the train station. The sounds of people bustling about is drowned out by the sound of my beating heart. The train station is busier today than it was before, at least thirty people are walking in and out and around the little building.

I stop abruptly.

"What is it, Birdie?"

"I'm not sure. Do you mind if we take a second to look around the train station? I'm just curious."

"Of course, come on."

We walk inside, and I take in the sights and sounds around me. It's odd I know, but there is a familiarity at being here. The low hum of people, the ticket window with an overly happy looking man working it, the posters on the walls of maps of train routes.

"Birdie, come here!"

I turn to my left and see Abrianna looking at something on the wall. I expect to see another map when something catches my eye. It is a golden plaque hanging on the wall. The plaque looks unusual, with intricate flower etchings framing the outside. Abrianna's eyes go wide as she points at the words written on the plaque. In big letters it reads:

BABY HOPE On June 3rd, 2000, Baby Hope was found abandoned at this train station. Where she came from is unknown but her impact on this community is substantial. We, the town of New Hope, PA., adopt Baby Hope. She will forever be our baby.

Above the gold plaque, encased in glass is a picture of Baby Hope, me, wrapped in a white towel. I am not sure I can describe for you, dear reader, how this makes me feel. I can say that I smiled, a warmth ran through my body, partially filling the empty cavity. The pieces of my heart coming back together.

Chapter Twenty-Four

The next couple of months at Alfred are a blur of class, coffee, and giggly nights with Abrianna. I don't make any headway with Austen and I only see him once in passing, the couple of pleading texts I send him get no response.

It is a perfect October day in Western New York, the leaves have changed colors, and the cool air is breezing through the campus creating a sense of magic. I have a book for class in hand and I am tucked under a large tree in the middle of campus. A wine-colored leaf drifts down from above, landing on the sleeve of my jacket. I brush it aside and take this moment to look around me. Students are meandering about, some sprinting with a purpose, clearly late for class, others taking their time. A couple is sitting on a bench just outside one of the dorms, kissing. I sigh as I think of Austen.

My phone buzzes in my pocket, it must be Abrianna but am surprised to see it is David.

I answer, reluctantly, "Hello?"

"Hi, Birdie? It's David Johnson. I hope you're doing well in college, I just wanted to give you the information on where you can go to get your DNA test done if you are still interested? I am sorry I have not arranged this sooner, I figured you would need a bit of time to get settled at school, plus I'm quite nervous about it myself if I'm honest."

"It's okay and yeah, I'm still interested."

"Great, I'll text you the address, it's the closest location I could get to your university."

"Thanks, David."

"I'll talk to you soon, Birdie."

I close my book. I can barely breathe, much less read. Part of me hoped he would not call. Part of me hoped that my time in New Hope was an apparition, a moment in time that I will never have to deal with again.

An overwhelming urge to cry sweeps over me and I put my head on my knees. I have managed to only cry a handful of times since my parents died, but it seems to be all I do lately. I need someone to talk to but Abrianna is in class.

Desperate, I call Austen. I have never called him before so he will surely be surprised.

I'm shocked when he answers, "Birdie? Why are you calling me?"

I sniffle and try desperately to pull it together, "I know that you don't want to be with me, Austen, but can we be friends at least? I need someone to talk to, I'm kind of overwhelmed right now."

"What's wrong, Birdie, why are you crying?"

"Please, can you meet me at my dorm?"

Austen sighs, "Okay, which dorm are you in?"

~~~

Twenty minutes later and Austen is knocking on my door. I can't believe he actually came. Maybe he does still care about me after all.

"Hey," I say as I open the door and let him in.

"Hi, look can we make this quick? It's weird for me to be here."

"I understand, I just need a friend right now and Abrianna is in class, so I thought of you."

"What's going on? Why are you crying?" Austen asks as he peels off his coat and sits on the bed, appearing nervous.

"Okay, well, it's a long story but, basically, I went to New Hope, Pennsylvania, with Abrianna a couple months ago. It's where I was born, to find out why I was abandoned as a baby."

Confusion sweeps across Austen's face, "Hold, on, what do you mean abandoned?"

"I never told you but when I was a baby, someone left me at a train station. Then I went into the foster care system."

"I thought you said your parents died in a car accident."

"They did, those were my adoptive parents, not my birth parents."

"Shit, are you serious?"

"Yes."

"Okay. So, you went there. Have you ever been back there since you were born?"

"No. I just wanted to see the place, plus, I had received a letter from the adoption agency a few years ago that a man living in New Hope was reaching out because he believed he may be my birth father. The letter had his contact information on it including his address. I didn't expect to find answers when I showed up unannounced, but I did."

"What'd you find out?"

"I believe my birth mother was Janet Marie, she had me when I was fifteen after she slept with the priest's, also fifteen-year-old, nephew. I met him. He is now the priest at the same church, and I look just like her, Austen, so much so that a lady a restaurant, a stranger, told me so."

"Hold on, you met the guy who could be your birth father?"

"Yes,"

"So why are you so upset right now if this was a couple months ago?"

"He just called me to give me the information about where to go to get a DNA test done and I'm just freaking

147

out. It feels too real, and I don't know what to do. I don't know if I really want to know the truth or not." I am pacing, arms crossed above my head.

"You should take the test, or you'll just spend your life wondering."

"I'm scared, though."

"What happened to your birth mother? Does she still live there?"

"No, she committed suicide on my thirteenth birthday."

"Holy cow, Birdie, are you serious?"

"Yes."

"Jesus, I'm so sorry. I don't know what to say. I'm not great at advice, Birdie, I mean I just don't know what to say."

"I just needed to talk about it, you don't have to say anything. It's been sitting on my chest heavily and when he called, it was like it started to crush me. I'm sorry to bring you into this, Austen."

"It's okay, but I'm not the person you should be talking to."

"We can't even be friends?"

"I don't think so."

"I understand, thanks for coming here and listening. I'm so sorry I ghosted you, Austen, I had such a great time that night, I just have problems. I'm hard to love," the tears are flowing freely now.

"Please Birdie, don't talk about that. I can't handle it."

"Can you give me another chance, Austen?" I am spiraling now, trying to grasp for him before I fall.

Austen stands up as if he has been jolted with electricity, "Please, don't say stuff like that to me," he is running his hands through his hair, "you're just upset right now. You don't mean what you're saying. You can't do this to me, you can't keep messing with my head. You need to know I've moved on. I had to. I have a girlfriend, so leave me alone."

No. "Really? A girlfriend? Already?!" I am screaming now.

Austen grabs his coat and runs out, leaving me with my second rejection.

Chapter Twenty-Five

The clinic is ten minutes away in a slightly bigger village than Alfred, in a town called Hornell. Abrianna drives me to the clinic and waits with me in the waiting room. I must be nervous because I am gripping my backpack in my lap so tightly that my knuckles have turned white.

"Elizabeth? You can come back now," says the too pleasant-looking woman, completely oblivious to the storm raging inside me. I stand up quickly and walk behind her and into the third room on the left.

"Have a seat over there for me, I am going to swab the inside of your cheek, and then you can leave. The sample will be sent to a lab and you will be notified of the results. It can take a little bit of time to get the results."

I am nodding frantically now, please just get this over with so I can leave.

"Open wide," the inside of my cheek is swabbed quickly and then the swab is put into a sealed container.

"Okay, we are all done."

"That's it?"

"Yes. It is a simple process."

"Okay, thanks," the words are barely out of my mouth and I am out the door.

~~~

It has been two days since I had my DNA test done and a week since my meltdown with Austen.

I need to vent so I call Abrianna, "Hey girl, what're you doin' right now?"

"I'm in my room working on my paper for my English class. Why? You okay?"

"Not really. I need someone to talk to, but I don't want

to burden you."

"Birdie, I'm a great listener and that is what friends are for. Come talk to me."

"Thanks, I'll be right there."

Abrianna knows something is up, but I haven't told her about Austen yet. It's just so embarrassing.

One hour and one box of tissues later, I finally feel a bit better, "Can you believe I made such a fool of myself in front of him? AGAIN. I could die."

"I don't think it's that bad, Birdie. Really, it tells me he isn't over you."

"Really? I was thinking the opposite."

"If he was over you, he wouldn't have answered your call, he wouldn't have come to your dorm room, and he wouldn't have gotten so upset when you tried to get him to take you back. That boy is very much in love with you."

"You're nuts!"

"Trust me girl, I know boys."

"Speaking of which, how's Evan?"

"Good," Abrianna smiles every time she hears his name, "we are exclusive ya know."

"That's amazing, how did it happen?"

"He told me he doesn't want me dating anyone else. It was that simple."

"Ha, I wish my love life was that simple."

"It will be, one day. Next time you're upset, talk to me instead of calling some ex-boyfriend."

"Deal. You know, Abrianna, you're the best friend I ever had, of course that isn't saying much as I haven't had lots of friends." We both laugh at this.

"That only makes it more special. Hey, let's make a pact."

"What?"

"Let's stay friends. The best of friends. I want you to

be the maid of honor at my wedding one day."

"Really? Me?"

"Hell yeah, I love you, girl."

"I love you, too."

"This is Insta worthy, Birdie," Abrianna says as she leans in close to me, snapping a picture as she does, "we need to get you online, girl."

"I don't know what I'd post."

"You have to be on social media, Birdie, it's weird not to be. Hand me your phone, let me hook you up."

"Fine, but I don't want to post much. Do you think Austen has an Instagram?"

"Duh."

"Have you seen it?" Abrianna quickly searches for Austen and it doesn't take but two seconds for her to find him.

"Here he is."

We scroll through his profile and it is mostly images of him with the guys from his high school football team and some recent ones from the football team at Alfred. My stomach drops as I see several pictures of him posing with beautiful women.

"I don't want to see this."

"Wait, Birdie, is that you?" Tucked away quietly without caption is a picture of me, laying on my back underneath the moonlight, laughing.

"When did he take this? You look amazing."

"I had no idea he took a picture of me that night. That's the night I smoked weed for the first time and we laid among the fireflies . . ."

"Damn, he's into you."

"Okay, I need a great profile pic, I want to get his attention."

"That 'a girl."

Chapter Twenty-Six

The holiday season has started, the loneliest time of the year for a girl like me. I received a letter in the mail from the lab last week, but I have yet to open it. Fear dictates my actions now as I am encased in it. What if he is my father? What if he is not?

All the other students have gone home for Thanksgiving break, leaving me here to wander the campus alone. Abrianna invited me to come home with her to Pennsylvania, but I declined, thinking at the time that being alone for a while would be good for me. Snow falls quietly over this quaint village, further compounding the loneliness. The snowflakes drift onto my shoulders and beanie as I make my way to the little grocery store to find something to eat for dinner, the letter from the lab stuffed in my coat pocket. I take it everywhere with me in case I become brave enough to open it. I plan to sleep all through Thanksgiving Day tomorrow, so I just need something to eat for tonight. It's so cold out that my nose feels frosted as the wind beats against it, the store is luckily just a few more strides away.

I feel a shake in my pocket and realize it is my phone, I pull it out to see that it is David calling me. I hit ignore. A few seconds later and he calls again, I stop walking and stare at the ringing phone, unsure of how to face this reality. I hit ignore again and lie to myself, telling myself I will call him once I am back in my dorm room.

He must know that I am ignoring him because he calls again immediately, I guess I will just have to face this after all.

I take a deep breath and answer, "Hi, David."

"Birdie, I'm so glad you picked up. Did you get the results? I got a letter a few days ago but wasn't brave enough to read it until this morning." Maybe this guy and

I are more alike than I thought.

"I have but I haven't read the results yet."

"Birdie, I don't know if you'll be happy with this or not, but I am your birth father."

I catch my breath in my throat, choking on it.

"Birdie, you okay? Are you upset?"

"I don't know how to feel."

"What are you doing for Thanksgiving?"

"I'm at the school, I'm an orphan remember? I don't have a family to go home to."

"You do now."

"What?"

"Birdie, I will buy you a train ticket so you can come down today, and then we can spend Thanksgiving together tomorrow."

"Why?"

"Because you are my daughter and I want to know you."

"Really?"

"Of course."

"Okay, um, I guess that's fine."

"Okay, I'll get you a train ticket and call you back with the details."

Spending Thanksgiving in New Hope with my birth father? A smile as big as the sky spreads across my face.

~~~

I step onto the platform and David, I mean my father, is sitting on the bench waiting for me. I am not comfortable with the idea yet, so I think I'll stick with calling him David.

"Hello, Birdie."

"Hi, David. Thanks for the ticket and the invite."

"Thanks for coming."

We walk the short walk to the church in silence, unsure about what to say to each other. It's comforting to know that he is just as unsure as me.

"I'll make lasagna for dinner tonight, then I have mass at nine. Would you come to mass with me?"

"Sure, I mean, I'm not religious but I don't mind."

"I'd love to have you there. Do you want people to know you are my daughter?"

"I don't know. Do you?"

"Yes. I want to share the news with my congregation."

"If you want to, that's fine with me."

~~~

The church is filled with people tonight and I am suddenly incredibly nervous about David's announcement. I pick a pew near the front like David requested and sit on the very edge. The church is lit up with candles, but all the people make it feel less ominous than it did the first time I was here.

It's the end of mass and time for David to share his news. He prepared me for this over dinner, telling me what he plans to say, but I'm nervous for him, I hope sharing this won't cause him any problems.

"On this glorious night," here it comes, "I have news to share with my congregation. I hope that you will welcome this news with open arms. I have one very important thing to be thankful for this year and I want to share this blessing with all of you. Many of you may recall that on June third, year 2000, Baby Hope was left at the train station in our small town. No one ever knew where Baby Hope came from or who left her at the station. Our great and lovely town of New Hope decided to wrap their arms around Baby Hope and, in a way, adopt her as our own. Well, it has been eighteen years now and I have some shocking news. After a surprising visit from a young lady late this summer, I had a DNA test done. That DNA test showed that this young lady was my daughter."

An audible gasp comes from the crowd.

"This young lady is the result of an intimate encounter I had at the young age of fifteen. I did not know the encounter resulted in the pregnancy but suspected it after Baby Hope was abandoned at the train station, some nine months later. I never spoke up. I kept this secret between myself and God. That was not right. I am not proud of that. I am, however, proud today to share with you all that I have a daughter and that Baby Hope has a name, Elizabeth Wright. I will not share with this congregation who Elizabeth's birth mother was because that is not my secret to tell. However, I ask that you all greet and welcome Baby Hope into your hearts and minds and forgive me, your priest, for not being perfect. If you think I should step down I will, but I ask you, and God, for forgiveness for my sins."

You could hear a pin drop.

David motions for me to stand up so I do. I turn to face the congregation and the crowd stands and begins to come towards me.

An elderly lady next to me is crying as she reaches for my hand, "Dear Baby Hope, I cried and prayed for you all these eighteen years. I'm so relieved to know who you are and that you're okay. This town has missed you and loved you since that day in June."

The next thirty minutes are a blur, but they consist of more hugs than I have ever received in my entire life combined. The warmth and welcome are uplifting, the cracks in my heart filling a bit more.

~~~

Thanksgiving is overrun with visitors, several even bringing us food for our meal. The front page of the local newspaper on Saturday is the picture of me as a newborn next to a picture of me the journalist got when he visited the house. The headline reads: **Baby Hope is Home.**

It's Saturday night when the doorbell rings, "Wow, another visitor? This late?" David opens the door and Stephanie from the diner is standing in the doorway.

"Stephanie, come in."

"Hello, Father Johnson."

"Please Steph, you have known me for years, call me David."

"Okay, thanks, I wasn't sure. Hi, Elizabeth," she says looking towards me.

"Hi, again."

"I just wanted to stop by and talk to you both for a few moments if you don't mind."

"Sure, have a seat Steph," David says as he motions her towards the couch.

Before she even sits, she blurts, "I know that your mother is Jane." Both David and I look to each other, unsure of what to say.

"How do you know?"

"I figured it out after I saw the newspaper headline. You just looked so much like Jane, and I know that Jane and David were intimate once."

"Did she tell you that, Steph?"

"Yes, I'm sorry, David. I hope this isn't too awkward for you. I know that you didn't want to reveal Elizabeth's mother's name, I won't tell anyone."

"It's okay, Steph. I'm not surprised that you know, I remember how close you two were, and please, call Elizabeth Birdie. That's what she goes by."

"Oh, sure. I'm actually here because I wanted to give you some pictures, Birdie. They are the only pictures I have of Jane, but I think they are meant for you. They are from the summers we spent as teenagers. She never told me that she had you, but Jane could be very private. I know that for a few months before you were found at the train station, she was acting a bit odd and had put on a touch of weight, but I never imagined she was pregnant. A few years later, she told me that she had slept with David but never said anything more about it. Anyway, I wanted you to have these." Steph hands me a small package with about ten pictures inside. I flip through them. They are all of Jane and Steph running along the beach. She looks so young.

"Thank you for this, Steph. I'm so glad you did this."

"You're welcome, dear. Your mother was a great woman, I loved her so much. I'm sorry she is not with us anymore, but I thought it was important for you to know how great she was and to give you these pictures.

If only I could have known her.

~~~

I hear a shuffling outside my door and know it must be David getting breakfast ready, the most important meal of the day. I'm not sure if that's true or not but he says it every morning.

"Is breakfast ready?" I yell from the small guest room.

"Birdie, can you come out here? You have a visitor." Another one? I cannot believe how many people want to meet me in this quaint town. I slip on my jeans and trusty Nirvana t-shirt before making my way out into the kitchen.

"Hello," I say to the elderly woman standing just by the kitchen table, I do not recognize her, and David has strange energy about him that makes me wary.

"Are you Baby Hope?" She asks in a small, weak

voice.

"Yes, my name is Elizabeth, but I go by Birdie. It's nice to meet you," I say as I get closer, holding out my hand.

The old woman looks down at my hand but does not attempt to shake it. The energy just keeps getting weirder.

"I'm Janet Marie's mother, Dorothea." *Shit.*

"Oh, I didn't realize."

"I know that you're Janet's daughter. I know she was the one who left the baby at the train station."

"How do you know?" My voice is shaking now. She pulls the chair in front of her and slowly sits down.

"I always knew. I knew she was pregnant. I knew she gave birth in the bathtub and I knew that the father was David. I was her mother; I knew everything about her."

"I thought she never told anyone, not even David."

"She didn't have to tell me I read it in her diary she kept under her pillow. Silly girl writing down such private thoughts." Dorothea's gray eyes match the grayness of her skin.

"Did she know you knew?"

"No, I never said anything to her. I was disappointed in her, in who she really was, I wanted her to live with the secret. Secrets have a tendency to destroy from the inside and that is what I wanted for her. She learned her lesson but made another disgraceful choice by taking her own life. I don't know where I went wrong with her, I think the devil had a hold of her."

My heart is so low in my body, it is weighing down my feet.

"Dorothea, that's not very Christian of you. What would Jesus have done?"

"Oh, shut up, David. You're no holy man. Having sex at fifteen and unwed. You're a disgrace to that church." David shuts up but glares at her in a way that is filled with hatred, something I would never have guessed he was capable of.

"I just came here to give you this suicide note Janet wrote since it pertains to you," she slides a piece of stained paper across the table towards me, "and to tell you to never come around to see me and never to go around telling people that Janet was your mother. I'm already ashamed enough by her suicide. I don't need you piling it on."

David and I just look at the woman, wrinkled with bitterness, until she stands back up and lets herself out.

"Birdie, please ignore Dorothea. She's a hateful woman. Always has been. Jane couldn't stand her. Your mother was nothing like her. Please don't take to heart anything she says. God loves you as do I. That's what matters." He loves me? Other than my adoptive parents, Austen, and Abrianna, no one has ever said that to me before.

I look down to the paper, "Can you read it to me?"

"Sure." David grabs the paper and begins, "Dear God, please forgive me. I can no longer live with the secret I have been keeping all these years. It has been eating me up inside. I am the one who abandoned Baby Hope. She was my child. I did not know what else to do, knowing that mine, and her father's lives would be ruined if anyone found out. Now, thirteen years later, my life is more ruined than if I would have raised her as my own. I miss her and think about her every day. I hope she is warm, safe, and loved. If by chance she ever sees this, I want her to know that I love her with every fiber of my being. Mostly, I want her to forgive me for leaving her and for taking my own life. Janet Marie."

"Why did she bring this here to give to me if she hated me so?" Tears flow freely, unabashed.

"Birdie, I don't know. She must know somewhere

deep in her heart that it was the right thing to do."

"I need to be alone," I race back into the bedroom.

Chapter Twenty-Seven

The next couple of weeks are cloudy, filled with cloudy skies and a cloudy heart. I am struggling to focus on anything, avoiding Abrianna, and any socializing completely. It's a dark winter night and it's snowing heavily as I read *Pride and Prejudice* again, desperately trying to find the answers amongst the pages. I give up and set it down on the blanket beside me. I wish I had my adoptive parents here instead of just this book. I miss them now more than ever. I grab my phone and pull up Instagram for the millionth time since Abrianna signed me up for it. I keep checking Austen's profile to see if he has taken down the picture of me, but he hasn't. However, as of a couple weeks ago, he has posted two pictures of him with some blonde. That must be her . . . the girlfriend.

"Birdie?" I jolt up in bed.

"Birdie, are you in there? It's Abrianna."

"Yeah, sorry. I'm here. Come in."

Abrianna opens the door and peeks her face inside, "Are you okay? I haven't talked to you in what feels like forever. Is something wrong? Did something more happen with David? Did you get your test results back?"

I sigh heavily, "My life is nuts. You want to come in and let me vent?"

Abrianna smiles, "You know it."

Twenty minutes later, Abrianna is understandably shocked, "First, wow. Second, shit. Third, Dorothea can suck it."

"Ha, thanks, Abrianna. I needed that."

"I'm telling you girl; your life is fascinating. The good news is that it sounds like your mother wanted you, she was just so young and had no support. I mean Dorothea would have been horrible. She loved you though, Birdie,

I can see that plain as day in reading this note she wrote. You shouldn't let one bad person make you feel bad about yourself. Plus, now you have some answers. That has to be nice, instead of not knowing."

"I know, you're right. Her words cut me like a knife, though. It's hard to get over, but yeah, I guess it is good to have answers. The not knowing was worse in a way. I just wish the story had a happier ending. I wish my mother hadn't committed suicide and I wish my grandmother wanted me around."

"I bet . . . but your dad wants you around. You know my parents had a rough go when they got together, being different religions and races and all. It did not go over well with their parents. But you know what they told me? They said that you can't choose who your parents are, and you are not your parents. You cannot choose where your DNA came from, Birdie, but that does not determine your life. That's up to you. You cannot change the way other people act. All you can do is change how you respond to them. Try not to focus on the one person giving you negativity about who you are, focus instead on the many sharing nothing but positivity, like the entire town of New Hope, your father, your mom's friend Steph, me, the list goes on."

I smile at Abrianna, maybe she is right. I had not thought about it in that way, why am I dwelling on one person's feelings when I have so many others that have been great?

"It must be nice to have a shrink as a mother, she always has great advice."

"Mostly, it's just really annoying." We laugh at this.

"Would it help a little if I changed the topic?"

"Sure, what's up?"

"It's about Austen. Listen, I don't know if you want to know this or not, but he and his girl broke up and Evan says that anytime he gets drunk, all he does is talk about you."

"Really? He still has pictures of her on his Instagram."

"Well, either way, they are over, Evan assures me of it . . . I think he misses you, Birdie. I don't think you should give up on him."

"But I screwed it up so badly."

"Yeah, but he obviously still loves you or he wouldn't talk about you when he's drunk."

"Maybe you're right. What should I do?"

"You should try to make it up to him, say you are sorry, tell him how you feel. Explain your situation."

"I already tried that and was brutally rejected, twice."

"Maybe it's time to try a new tactic then. Evan says they are having a party tomorrow night to celebrate the end of their season. Why don't you get all dolled up and come? See if you can make him jealous."

"Make him jealous? I wouldn't have a clue how to do that."

"I will help. I'm great at it."

"Can I borrow something of yours to wear?"

"Of course, this is the not the night for a Nirvana t-shirt, Birdie, we are going for sexy here."

I doubt it's possible to make Austen jealous, he is probably too hung up on his ex-girlfriend, but I guess it can't hurt at this point. Hell, what's one more embarrassing encounter?

~~~

It is nine p.m. on a Saturday when I knock on Abrianna's door, she swings it open, Kygo is playing in the background, and she looks as beautiful as ever as her curls bounce while she dances.

"Birdie! Come in! Have a glass of Moscato and let's

get you looking sexy!"

"HA! Yes, please."

Three outfits later, we finally land on the winner. A silver shimmery loose-fitting tank top that Abrianna swears make my brown eyes pop, a pair of tight black jeans, and strappy sandals. Not exactly winter appropriate, but I must say, I don't look half bad. Abrianna braids my hair into a loose French braid and completes the looks with a couple of streaks of sparkly green eye shadow.

"If Austen doesn't get a boner for you in this outfit, then there is no hope for the boy." I laugh, gaze at my reflection, surprised by the grown-up person looking back at me.

We grab our purses and coats and sprint down to the football house, the same white Victorian we partied in the first week on campus. When we walk in, loud electronic music hits my ears transporting me to another world.

I make my way through the crowd, searching for Austen's face amongst them. I finally spot him, leaning back against the wall with a beer in hand, another hand in his pocket, and a beautiful brunette standing way too close to him. He is flashing her his best smile and my hopes at rekindling are dashed. Instead of approaching, I grab the first beer I come across and chug it. I will just try to have fun and forget about him.

I trace back my steps and find Abrianna who is already locking lips with Evan in the kitchen. I better not interrupt.

"Hey, aren't you in my psych class? Nirvana girl, right?"

I turn to see a tall, very handsome blond with glasses standing in front of me. His nerdy look combined with his muscular body is somewhat off-putting.

"Um, yeah. I'm Birdie. And you are?"

"Dillon, it's nice to meet you." Dillon sticks out his hand for a shake and I embrace it, feeling the warmth of his hand against mine.

"So, you must be a huge Nirvana fan."

"Oh yeah, they're my favorite band." I should really listen to some more songs of theirs if I am going to keep wearing that shirt, I only know the two Austen put on my phone.

"I love them too, my older sister used to listen to them all the time back in the day. Can I get you another drink?"

"Sure," is this guy flirting with me? It is hard for me to tell, having worked so hard to keep people away for so long, I missed how to pick up on those kinds of social cues. I turn back to Abrianna who is nodding at me fervently, encouraging me to go for it.

Dillon hands me a can of Bud Light, which is disgusting by the way, and asks me to join him on the living room couch. Knowing that will be in the eyesight of Austen, I go, hoping to enact the jealously plan.

~~~

Dillon is smart. Smart and hot. It is a crazy good combination, but all my dumbass can think about is Austen. I can practically *feel* Austen's gaze on my back. I know he is seeing this interaction, so I am sure to lean in close to Dillon as he talks about psych class.

After a while of flirting, Dillon startles me as he presses his lips to mine. I push him away immediately. A couple of seconds go by, but he comes right back, kissing me again, so I push him away again.

"I'm sorry, but I don't want to do this."

"Whatever, you've been flirting with me for like an hour. What's your problem?"

"I'm just not interested, sorry. I didn't mean to give you the wrong idea."

"Look, I didn't just waste all this time talking to you for nothing," Dillon says as he puts his hand in between my legs and rugs my inner thigh. I push his hand away and get ready to stand up when I notice Dillon looking confusedly at something behind me.

"What do you want, dude?"

"Get away from her." I turn to see a very red-faced Austen.

"This is none of your business, back off."

"She already told you once that she is not interested so get up and leave. Now."

"Who the hell are you to tell me what to do?"

"Get away from her before I punch you, dude."

Dillon gets up, "Whatever, I don't need this. There are plenty of other chicks, hotter ones, too."

I stand up and turn to Austen who is staring down at me, "You okay, Birdie?"

"Austen, why did…" Austen is walking off before I can even finish the statement. Austen goes upstairs and I race behind, calling after him. Apparently, I never learn.

"Please, stop following me, Birdie. Leave me alone."

"Austen, stop. Why did you just do that? I wanna talk to you. Please."

Austen opens the door to the side room, and I barge inside after him. He sits on the bed and looks at the floor.

"Birdie, I told you, I don't want to talk to you."

"I know, I don't want to bother you, Austen. Thanks for helping me out down there."

Austen looks up at me, pain etched across his face, "Why were you talking to that guy in front of me? Was it on purpose?"

"Um, well, Abrianna suggested I try to make you jealous."

"Well, congrats, it worked. I wish you would stop torturing me Birdie."

"I don't want to torture you. I just want to make up for what I did."

"I don't know, I don't think you can. I was so . . . I've never said anything like that to a girl before, and then you just . . . I don't even like to think about it."

I sit on my knees in front of him, wrapping my hands in his, searching his eyes, "Austen, forgive me please." I lean up and kiss him gently, he hesitates so I keep kissing him, hoping he will let go and kiss me back.

He puts his arms around me and lifts me up, so I am sitting on his lap, "Damn, Birdie." Austen kisses me hard, running his tongue against mine, my heart beating against my chest.

I break contact, "Is it true that you get drunk and talk about me?"

Austen grabs my head to bring it back to him, "You aren't supposed to know about that. Evan's a dead man."

"Don't, I'm glad to know. I think about you all the time." Austen looks unsure as his hazel eyes are on me, he responds by kissing me again.

Daringly, I push Austen back slightly, giving myself just enough room to pull the sparkly tank top up over my head. Austen's jaw is clenched, and I can tell he is still unsure, so I reach back and unhook my bra, letting it drop to the floor.

It's enough for Austen to overcome his uncertainty and he flips me over onto my back and hovers over me, quickly tugging his shirt over his head with one arm. His turtle necklace dangles above me.

Austen runs his lips down my neck and onto my chest, nipping my skin as he goes. Once he makes it down to the bottom of my jeans, he undoes them and pulls them off me, taking my underwear with them. Suddenly very aware of my nudity, I try to cover up with my arms.

"Don't do that," Austen grabs me by the wrists and holds them above my head, "have you done this with anyone else?"

"No, just you."

"Good." Austen surprises me with his possessiveness but I can't help but love it. He pulls a condom out of his back pocket and tears the edge with his teeth.

"Who were you saving that for?" Apparently, I can be possessive, too.

"You."

With a quick motion, Austen is inside me, the sharp pain from the first time is back but only lasts a moment, soon that pain turns to pleasure.

We melt into each other. The slight smell of Irish Spring, the turtle necklace swinging back and forth, solidifying into memory.

The words I love you keep rolling around my head, but I can't get the courage to say them because, fear, my old companion, refuses to leave my side.

~~~

I wake up and it's early, the day is just beginning to streak through the window blinds, casting a soft light across this strange room. I turn to Austen, but the pillow beside me is empty.

Chapter Twenty-Eight

Austen fled in the night. I never woke, he snuck away without making a sound. After the first time I had sex, I fled, the second, he did. I am not having very good luck in the sex department. I can still smell him on me when I make my way outside, his scent filling my nose as I pull my scarf up to cover my mouth and nose from the bite of the morning frost.

His leaving has left me a shell of a person, but I must forge on as if I am okay. That is something you grow good at as a foster kid, pretending to be okay when you're not. I get back to my dorm and see a piece of paper taped to the outside, I pull it off and unlock the door, shedding my scarf and coat once inside. The note is from Abrianna: *Come see me when you get back.*

I race over to Abrianna's room, she swings the door open and smiles wide, "Is it true?"

"Is what true?" I ask, genuinely unsure about what she is talking about.

"That you and Austen hooked up last night?"

"Oh god, how do you know about that?"

"Everybody knows, it was the talk of the night. You were seen going with him into one of the bedrooms. Did you? Did you stay with him? Was it great?"

"It was great, yes. But he snuck out this morning without saying goodbye. I don't think he's ready to forgive me."

"Oh, I'm sorry, Birdie, but at least you're on the right track. In no time, you two will be a couple, I guarantee it."

"How was your night?"

"It was okay, but I think something's up with Evan," Abrianna is smiling but appears nervous.

"How so?"

"I dunno, I can't put my finger on it. He just seemed distant. I'm probably overthinking it."

"Why don't you ask him about it?"

"Maybe, I just hope we're okay."

"I'm sure you are, he is mad over you."

"I hope so."

"Be grateful, Abrianna, at least you're not in love with a guy who used to think you were creepy," I say trying to make her laugh.

Abrianna laughs and shakes her head at me, amused by me, "You are one strange girl, Birdie."

"That's what I keep hearing."

Chapter Twenty-Nine

Thanks to the personal upheaval of my life, I am struggling a little bit in a couple of my classes, and now I have no choice but to do well on my finals or I could lose my scholarship.

One of the classes that I need to do well in is an art class. It's just an intro class and I took it thinking it would be fun and easy. It has turned out to be much harder than I expected, the professor is an art Nazi and expects all of us to produce Mona Lisas even though this is just an intro class. I must do well on the final big art project to keep a B in the class and therefore, keep my GPA where it needs to be.

Today, Professor Art Nazi has us choose what medium we want to use for our final project, and I choose oil on canvas even though I have no real reason to, as I am not good at any of the mediums. We are also to pick a topic for the final, I choose happiness. Maybe if I paint something that reminds me of happiness, I can force myself to be happy.

~~~

Suddenly, the first semester of my college experience is about over. The days have gone by in a flash, a mix of happiness at finally being here and sadness at the undercurrent of turmoil in my heart.

I need to focus on my finals. The last thing I want to do is fail out of my dream college. It is so difficult, though, because I have such a hard time concentrating; my body and mind running between New Hope and Austen, never getting any rest.

Tonight, I need to complete my final art project, so I grab the canvas and oil paints and pack them into my backpack annoyed that I have to do this. I wish I had never taken this class. I don't know why I took it to begin with, my artistic abilities are minimal at best. The snow crunches beneath my feet and the night sky glitters above as I make my way to the art studio, thinking that I will be able to focus more if I paint there than in my dorm room.

Once inside, I pick a chair and easel closest to one of the large windows, hoping to draw inspiration from the night sky.

I have no idea what to paint, what makes me happy?

I pick up a paintbrush and prepare the paints, still not knowing what I am going to do when a twinkle draws my eye back to the window, back to the stars. They are bright tonight, reminding me of that summer night here with Austen.

With sudden inspiration, I begin.

~~~

When I turned in my painting in the morning, I do so expecting little to no fanfare from Professor Art Nazi.

It is now the last day of the semester and grades are posted. I log in to the library computer to check my grade, hoping my painting got at least a C. My head spins because instead of a C, I see an A. Professor *Not As Bad As I Thought* leaves a comment beside it: "Elizabeth, great job on your final project, the magic of your painting and the heart you poured into it is evident. I would like to hang your painting in the show I am putting together for display for next semester. If you have any issues with this, please reach out."

Wow.

~~~

I can't believe it is already Christmas break, one semester down.

Alfred is wonderful. The place is magical, and the professors are brilliant. It is truly everything I could have dreamed of and more. My happiness at being here has an undercurrent of stress and unease, though. Losing Austen, the pain of everything I have learned about my birth mother and the rejection from Dorothea runs like a river through my heart and mind, flowing through my subconsciousness. I have not spoken to Austen once since that night we shared, I have seen him around at a party or two but as soon as I show up, he leaves.

For winter break, I am going back to New York City to stay at Liza and Aiesha's place for a week and I am bringing Abrianna with me. Abrianna will then head home to Pennsylvania and me to New Hope. We were going to drive Abrianna's car, but her parents don't want her to drive in the City, so they bought us both train tickets to get to the city instead.

I open the suitcase David gave me (yes, my first suitcase!) and put a few shirts, including my trusty Nirvana t-shirt, the picture of my birth mother, some of the makeup that Abrianna gave me, and my copy of *Pride and Prejudice* with Jane's suicide note safety tucked inside the pages. I snap the bottoms and race out the door to catch a ride to the train station from Abrianna, she is waiting for me in the lobby.

"Hurry up, girl! We have to get on the road!"

We hop into her car, blast the music, and head to the train station.

~~~

A long day of travel later, we finally pull in front of Liza and Aiesha's apartment. They are waiting, standing

174

outside smoking cigarettes.

"Birdie!"

"Hey! I'm so glad to finally be here, I've missed you girls!" Well, Aiesha at least.

We embrace just as Malcolm walks up, "Hey Birdie, my girl!" He joins in the group hug.

"You must be the amazing Abrianna," Aiesha is hugging Abrianna, welcoming her, "I'm so glad that you came! This is going to be one fun week."

~~~

"So, you met your dad, your evil grandmother, and the entire town of New Hope is like obsessed with you? I want to go to this place, it sounds nutty." Malcolm is three martinis in, it is the first time I have ever seen him drunk, and I am loving it.

"Yes, to all of that. It's been wild."

"What about Austen? Is he still not talking to you?"

"No, I don't know how to get him to forgive me, Malcolm."

"He might not forgive you, Birdie. I mean, he told you he loved you and you fled the other direction. That's rough. I mean, he's not the type to share his feelings like that."

"Ugh, I know, I know."

"He was always sharing his feelings with me. He was obsessed with me for years," Liza says as she places a record on her teal blue record player.

"Did he tell you he loved you?" Malcolm asks Liza boldly. My organs melt as I wait for her reply.

"All the time. I would snap my fingers and he would come running, but I was never really interested in him. He is just kind of blah, but that sounds perfect for you, Birdie."

Malcolm rolls his eyes, "Whatever, Liza, Austen is hot. But you, Birdie, are out of his league. I hope you know that."

"I think she still has a chance," I can always count on Abrianna's optimism.

"Miss Abrianna, I love you and your attitude, but I think you are wrong about this. I don't think that boy will ever recover from such embarrassment."

"Oh, stop, Malcolm, you're being overly dramatic about it," Aiesha says with a handful of potato chips shoved in her mouth.

"Of course, I'm gay, I'm always dramatic."

"It doesn't count until Mom and Dad know."

"You still haven't told them, Malcolm?" I ask, encouraging the topic change.

Malcolm rolls his eyes, "I will. Soon. But not yet. They are not ready to hear it yet. Why don't we call Austen and invite him to the party?"

"What? No!" I exclaim, not wanting to make things worse between Austen and me.

"Why not, we won't tell him you are here, we will pretend that we don't even know you all have hooked up. We'll play dumb and it'll give you a chance to try one more time."

"I don't hate the idea." Great, now Aiesha is in on it.

"I think he'll be pissed."

"No way. He loves you. He'll be glad to see you." Damn Abrianna and her optimism.

~~~

Three hours later and the tempo of the room has risen significantly thanks to drunk people and music. I have had one too many drinks, but I needed to build up my nerve because Austen said he might stop by when Liza insisted on being the one to text him. I hope he doesn't think it's because she wants to hook up.

I have started to see double so I better chill, I grab the couch for support and ease myself down, hoping I look more put together than I am. The crowd of partygoers creates a blurry scene in front of me, the only objects staying still are me and the couch. My body is warm but numb thanks to the alcohol and all I can think about is how I wish Austen would walk in and hold me.

One of the blurry objects in front of me stops and bends down, it's Malcolm, "Birdie, he's here."

I nod and look behind him, desperate to see Austen's form. I spot a man with a too tight of fitting, black shirt coming towards me, it's him.

"Birdie? I didn't know you were going to be here."

I stand awkwardly, "I'm sorry, Austen. Is this okay?"

"Yeah, I guess." Austen takes a big gulp of beer and continues, "Actually, is there somewhere we can talk?"

"Yeah, follow me." I lead Austen to the room that I am sharing with Aiesha, motioning him towards the blow-up mattress on the floor.

"That's my bed for the week, Abrianna's on the couch."

"Cool," Austen sits, I stand a distance away not wanting to scare him off.

"Listen, Birdie, I'm sorry for bailing after last time . . . that was pretty shitty of me. It wasn't right and I just wanted to say sorry."

"You don't need to apologize, Austen. I understand why you did it. It's no worse than me ghosting you the way I did. Does this make us even now and you can forgive me?"

"Hmmm, do you think we could be just friends? I wouldn't mind that if you want. Just friends, though, I don't want anything more."

My heart rips open, "Yes, of course, friends would be great," I grab the dresser for support, Austen thinks it is because I drank too much but it is to support my broken heart.

"You okay, Birdie? I think you drank too much. You better drink some water, or it is going to be a rough day for you tomorrow."

"I'm okay," I say, desperate to keep it together, "can I ask you something?"

"What?"

"Did you used to tell Liza you loved her all the time?"

"What? NO. Did she say that?" I nod, "She would. I never said that to her. I have only ever said it to one girl one time," Austen pauses suddenly remembering who he is talking to, "forget it."

Desperate to change the topic I ask, "What's that necklace about anyways? Why a turtle? I've always wanted to know."

"Oh," Austen grabs the turtle and looks at it, "my grandma gave it to me when I was a kid. She bought it for me after she took me to the zoo. She said I went on and on about this big turtle that was there, some hundred-year-old guy. I don't remember that specifically, but she did. She got me this necklace because she thought turtles are my favorite animal or something."

"Are they?"

"No, not at all. I think my favorite animal is a lion. I don't know why I got so excited 'bout that one turtle at the zoo. I was only five, though."

"You wear it a lot."

"I wear it because it reminds me of her, not because of the turtle, I mean turtles are cool, though."

"Did she pass away?"

"She did, two years ago. She was the only person in my life who I felt was genuine. Most of the people I know are so fake. Fake parents, fake friends. Well, other than you."

"You think I am genuine?"

"Definitely. That's why I want to keep you as a friend."

"That sounds good to me, Austen," I say, meaning it but wishing for more.

Austen stands up, his height overwhelming me, "Sweet, let's get out there and have some fun."

~~~

Do you know those few perfect nights that you go back to as an adult over and over again? Those few nights where you are completely young and alive? Growing up in the system, I only dreamed of such things, but tonight, here in New York City, crammed into a tiny apartment with some of the best people I have ever known, dancing and laughing, I get to live it.

We are two drinking games in and Abrianna and Aiesha are deep in a political debate while Liza is kissing her new, surprisingly young, boyfriend, and Malcolm, Austen, and I are dancing to Malcolm's favorite Prince record he's playing on the vinyl record player. Time seems to slow as we jump up and down to *Purple Rain*, the sight of Austen's toothy grin and turtle necklace floating in the air burns into my brain, adding to my growing collection of enchanted moments.

The room is alive with the sounds of laughter and music and if a heart could smile, mine would. Happiness, I'm learning, is a lot of things. It's laughter, dancing, friendship, and love. It's also little things like vinyl records and fireflies.

Chapter Thirty

I wake up in pain, my head throbbing as I crawl out of bed to get some water. Partying with Aiesha and Liza and Malcolm might be more than I can handle. I inch my way into the living room and see Austen sprawled on the floor with a pillow, his shirt lifted showing his beautiful stomach, his necklace falling to side. I would give anything to be able to touch him again.

A sudden cry jolts Austen awake, "What the hell was that? Was that you, Birdie?"

"No, I think it was Abrianna," Austen stands, and we run back into the bedroom, Aiesha is sitting next to Abrianna trying to comfort her.

"Abrianna, what's wrong?"

"He broke up with me."

"What?"

"Evan, he texted me and I didn't see it until this morning. It says, I'm sorry but I can't see you anymore. Forgive me."

~~~

Abrianna cries the entire rest of the week. All day, every day. To see her this devastated is horrible. I sit by her side and try to do everything I can to cheer her up, but nothing works. Austen and Malcolm both come by every day to see how she is doing.

It's Thursday afternoon when I hear a knock on the door, Austen and Malcolm are here.

"Hey, Birdie, we just wanted to stop by and see how Abrianna is doing," Austen says as I motion them both inside.

"She's sleeping. I'm so pissed at Evan. How could he do this to her?"

"He's a moron, she's amazing."

"I know."

"Would you guys want to get some food? I was wondering if you would come with me to Charlie's."

"Charlie's? You sure 'bout that, Malcolm?"

"Yeah, I think so, but I could use the support if you don't mind coming with me."

"Why, what's up bro?"

"There's this guy, Marcus, he works there, and I haven't stopped thinking about him since the summer. We kissed once and then I ruined it. I wanna see if he will give me another chance. I kinda blew it."

Austen glances to me quickly, "I'm down."

"Me too, of course. Let me see if Abrianna wants to come."

~~~

Abrianna opts out, she just wants to sleep so I promise to bring her back some pizza. Charlie's looks the same, the checkered table clothes and the owners are still Italian and grumpy.

"Do you know if he still works here, Malcolm?"

"Oh yeah, I drive by sometimes."

"Creeper."

"You're one to talk." Austen smiles as he says this.

We pick a booth in the back as Malcolm looks around for Marcus, trying not to appear obvious about it.

The same man from the first time I was here comes up and tells us what we are having, "Today, it's pepperoni. I'll bring two larges out."

"Thanks man, hey, is Marcus working today?"

"He's on break, he'll be right back."

"What're you gonna say, Malcolm?"

"I'm sorry? Do you still like me? That's all I can come

up with."

"Sounds perfect to me," Austen says as he tries to be helpful.

I tease him, "You're one to talk." This time it's me that's smiling.

Marcus spots Malcolm immediately, but doesn't come over. Malcolm waves him over.

"What do you want?"

"Hey, um, do you think we could step outside to talk for a minute?"

"No, I'm busy."

"Okay, okay, I will just say it now then. Marcus, I'm sorry. Do you still like me because I really like you. In fact, I haven't stopped thinking about you since we kissed."

Joy is the only word I can think of to describe Marcus's face, "Really? Yeah, definitely."

"I wish it was that easy for me," I say, leaning into Austen.

Austen smiles, "Friends, remember?"

"Friends."

~~~

It's now Friday and we are supposed to take the train in the morning.

Austen just walked in, "Hey Birdie, are you still going to leave tomorrow?"

"That's the plan but I'm worried about her."

"Why don't I drive you guys instead of you all taking the train? Doesn't she live in Pennsylvania? I can take her. That way maybe we can cheer her up. Road trips can be good for that."

"That's so nice of you, Austen, but that would be way too much for you to do, you would be driving back on

Christmas day."

"I don't mind. I don't have anything going on. My parents are both going to be out of town for Christmas anyway so it's no big deal."

"What do you mean? You're going to be all by yourself on Christmas?"

"Yeah, it's no big deal." As a girl who has spent many holidays alone, I know that's not true.

"Let me check with Abrianna and see what she wants to do."

I open the bedroom door quietly, Abrianna is curled up on the mattress, "Abrianna? Listen, Austen offered to drive us tomorrow if you're up for it. He doesn't mind, he doesn't have any plans for Christmas I guess."

Abrianna turns to me, her eyes red, "Is that what you want to do?"

"Hmm, it might be fun to go on a road trip and I won't lie, I'd love to spend some more time with Austen. Maybe it will cheer you up, come on Abrianna, let's have some fun."

She sniffles, "Fun sounds great and I've never been on a road trip."

"Great, let me call David and see if he's okay with Austen staying with us for Christmas, I can't bear the thought of him being alone in that house."

"Good idea, I wouldn't want that either."

Chapter Thirty-One

The idea of going on a road trip might have sounded fun, but December in New England has made it not such a good idea.

We are just outside of New York City when the snow starts falling, "This might get interesting," Austen says as he leans forward looking towards the darkening sky.

"I guess we should've checked the weather first," Abrianna bellows from the back. She is still in her pajamas but is just as beautiful as ever as she shovels Oreos in her mouth. I can tell she is starting to feel better.

"Yeah, we're dumb."

It only takes thirty more minutes for us to realize that we are going to have to stop somewhere and stay the night. Snow is drifting across the interstate, covering the dotted lines, preventing Austen from even being able to tell if he is still on the road or not.

Abrianna looks up the closest exit with a hotel on her phone, "Okay, two miles for exit fifteen. There is some motel there."

"I'll get us a couple of rooms. My parents can pay for this since they left me at Christmas. I'll consider this their way of saying sorry," Austen's knuckles are white as he grips the steering wheel.

I'm sweaty and shaking, the thought of my adoptive parents dying in a car crash is at the forefront of my brain. Two miles feels like twenty, but we finally make it to the exit and pull into a ratchet-looking motel.

"Yikes, is this place haunted or something?" Abrianna asks.

With a 'rooms available' sign lit up and only one other car in the parking lot, I'm getting a Shining vibe, "Scary, let's just get inside, hopefully it's not too disgusting."

"Should be cheap at least," Austen says, laughing.

~~~

I am sitting on top of the bed sheets because this is not the type of place you want to sleep underneath them. My coat will have to suffice to keep me warm.

It's nearing midnight and Abrianna and I have been gorging on snacks from the vending machine and gossiping, "Okay, enough of this, Birdie. Why are you in here with me when you know darn well that Austen is waiting for you in his room?"

"No, he isn't, Abrianna. He told me he just wants to be friends. A couple times, actually."

"Why don't you knock and find out for sure."

"Because he will reject me again and I can't take anymore rejection."

"Sure you can, it won't kill you. If it killed people, I'd be dead right now."

"Oh god, I dunno. What would I say?"

"Just knock and ask if you can come in."

"Fine. But this is the last time I am going to try anything with him."

"Sure it is . . . he is obviously crazy about you, why do you think he would drive you and your sad friend around?"

"I have no idea."

"Well, why don't you go find out."

I get up and glance at myself in the mirror, pinching my cheeks to bring some life back into my face. When I step outside, the white monster accosts me and even though I am only outside for a couple of seconds, I am blanketed in its snowy debris.

"Birdie? Come in, what're you doing? You look like a snowman."

I shiver as I try to explain, "I just wanted to see what you were up to."

185

"Oh, okay, sit down. I was just watching a movie."

I crawl onto his bed and under his coat to warm up, "Here, I'll warm you up."

Austen sits down on the bed beside me and wraps his arms around me. I lean back against his chest.

"This is dangerous, Birdie."

I lift my chin to look back at him, "Why?"

"It's hard for me to resist you when you're this close to me." He is breathing erratically now, and he is chewing on his lip tensely.

"Then don't." My boldness surprises me.

Austen's eyes go wide, and he glances to my mouth. He hesitates but leans down and kisses me. The warmth of his lips against the coolness of mine sends tingling sensations to the tips of my toes. Austen's tongue grazes mine and I turn to jelly.

He pulls back suddenly, "I'm sorry, Birdie. I can't."

"Did I do something wrong?"

"No, it's just that I got back together with Mia." Oh no.

"You did? When?

"Right before winter break."

"Why?"

"I dunno, I just like her." Like, but not love, thank God.

"You're never going to forgive me, are you?"

Austen sighs, "I have forgiven you, Birdie. I just think we're better as friends. I don't think you understand how much you hurt me. I really can't go through that again."

I bite my lip to fight back tears, "I understand, Austen. I want you to be happy and if you want to just be friends, then I get it."

Austen runs his finger under my chin, "Please let me go, Birdie." *Never.*

"Okay . . . but only if you spend Christmas with me."

186

"What?"

"Come and spend Christmas with me in New Hope. I can't stand the idea of you being alone on Christmas."

"Will your dad be okay with that?"

"Yeah, I called him already. He said it's fine as long as you sleep on the couch."

"Ha. Okay, sure, why not. Thanks for the invite . . . friend."

"No problem . . . friend."

~~~

The blizzard ends and once the plow goes by, we are back on the road. By dinnertime, Abrianna is home and Austen and I are in New Hope.

David opens his front door, "Welcome!"

"Hi, David. Thanks for having us. This is my friend Austen."

"Thanks for coming. Austen, it's nice to meet you, please come inside."

"Nice to meet you too, Father Johnson."

"No, please call me David. Are you hungry? I'm not much of a cook, well other than lasagna, but Rhonda, a member of the congregation, is an excellent cook. She put together a few dishes for us out of the kindness of her heart. She's a good Christian woman."

"That's nice of her, we're starving"

That evening we share good food and some laughs while we play Monopoly, a game that David has never played before, but a lady at his church let him borrow for tonight. Austen sleeps on the couch, as promised, and I lay in the guest room unable to sleep, the kiss from last night and *let me go* incessantly run through my head all night long.

~~~

It's Christmas morning and the smell of bacon wakes me up. I pull back the blinds. It's a snowy day, staining the town white. I slip on the robe David let me borrow and creak the door open just a hair to see if I can tell if David or Austen are awake yet.

I hear David, "Birdie? Are you up?"

"Yeah, I smell bacon."

"Mornin'," Austen says looking disheveled, sleepy, and glorious.

"Birdie, I put your gift on the kitchen table. We can have breakfast after you open it."

"Okay, thanks, hold on, I need to grab your gift." I turn back and get a small present from my backpack.

"You didn't have to get me anything, Birdie."

"It's not much."

I hand David the gift, he is sitting on his couch, already in his garb. I do not think I have seen him wear anything else, "Thanks Birdie, do you want me to open it now?"

"Yeah, go ahead." David opens the bag and I hold my breath in anticipation. It was tough to come up with an idea, but Malcolm said I should give him a framed picture of me. Abrianna took the picture of me sitting on Aiesha's couch and Aiesha gave me an old frame of hers, a silver one with a small scrape on the bottom.

"Oh my, thank you so much. This is perfect. I was wanting a picture of you to show people, I mean, other than the one in the newspaper."

"Really? You like it?"

"I love it. Now open mine."

I grab the gift off the small kitchen table and tear off the wrapping quickly.

Aaanndd it's a bible. Oh boy, I should have figured.

"Oh, thank you, David."

"It's not what you think, Birdie. Open up the front cover."

I flip the front cover and see an inscription. It reads: *To my dear David. This was my grandmother's before she gave it to my father. It is the only thing I own of my father's, but I want you to have it. Mother does not want it in the house anymore, but I want to give it to someone who will use it and love it as I much as I do. Love, Jane.*

My heart melts, "Thank you, David. It means more to me than I can even say," I say as I fight back tears.

~~~

Having Austen in my life as a friend might seem like a bad idea because it is. Spending time with him only deepens my love for him. It's the day after Christmas and Austen is getting in his car to make his drive back home and my heart strings reach out to his, hoping to keep him near me.

"Wait, Austen, can I have a hug? Friends hug."

"Sure, Birdie," I hold on tightly, not wanting to let go.

"Listen, Birdie, I got you a Christmas present."

"You did? Why didn't you give it to me yesterday?"

Austen shrugs. "I wish I would've gotten you something. What is it?"

Austen pulls out a small box from his pocket, "It's no big deal, I just thought of you when I saw it."

I open up the simple black cardboard box. It's a necklace with a small pendant on the end. It is a book with *Pride and Prejudice* written in tiny script across it. It's the cutest necklace I have ever seen and that includes Austen's turtle necklace.

"Oh, Austen, I love it."

"It's not a big deal, okay? It was like twenty bucks."

"Thank you," I look up into his eyes, wishing now more than ever that he would stop fighting this and just love me. He is uneasy as he looks down at me, biting his lower lip.

"I have to go. Enjoy the rest of your break," Austen is in his car driving away before I have a chance to respond, leaving a trail of smoke behind.

Chapter Thirty-Two

It's noon and I am sitting in the cafeteria waiting for Austen and Abrianna. Austen is taking this whole friend thing seriously and has lunch with us regularly now. I find it to be torture, but I digress. Abrianna sits down and she is flushed.

"What's wrong?"

She is holding her breath, "Austen is bringing his girl to lunch today, I saw him just outside with her and he said they'd be right in, if you leave now, I'll make up some excuse," her words come racing out.

Crap-on-a-cracker. "No, I don't want to leave, that'll just be obvious."

"Okay, I'll be here with you. Try not to think about it too much."

I focus on the food in front of me when Austen walks up with a beautiful blonde. Ugh. Of course, she is beautiful.

"Hey guys, this is Mia."

She waves and smiles. I wish I could punch her.

"Hi Mia, I'm Birdie, this is Abrianna."

"Hey, y'all!" *Y'all??*

"She's from Texas. Isn't that wild?"

"Cool," says Abrianna, but I can tell she is not impressed.

"Hey! I see you in the library all the time, like every time I go there."

"Oh, yeah, I'm there a lot."

"But why? I only go there if I have to."

"Um, I use their computers."

"Why?" God, I hate this chick.

"Because I don't have a computer of my own."

"Aw, that's so sad." Abrianna shoots Mia an angry glare.

I notice Austen has his hand on her thigh and it makes me want to play in traffic so I think it might be a good time to get up and get a coffee refill.

Standing at the coffee station, Austen taps my shoulder, startling me, "Hey, Birdie."

"Hey, Austen."

"Is it okay that I brought her?"

"Of course."

"Okay, because I meant it when I said I wanted to be friends."

"I know you did and so do I."

"You dating anyone?"

"Kind of."

"Yeah? Who? Do I know him?"

"It's not important right now. I will tell you about it if it gets more serious."

"Okay, thanks for being cool, Birdie."

"Sure." So, cool, I just told him I about an imaginary boyfriend. Yup, reeeallly cool, Birdie.

~~~

"You told him you were seeing someone?"

"I am not proud of it, Abrianna, I don't even know why I did that." I am running my hands through my hair now, my anxiety tugging on the strands.

"Birdie, I know guys who like you. Why don't you let me set you up with someone? I promise it'll be with someone cool. Plus, if you date someone, Austen would get so jealous."

"I don't want to make him jealous. I just want him."

"I know but sometimes you have to play the game, girl."

"That got me nowhere with him, remember?"

"Not true at all, it got you laid."

"Abrianna!"

"Oh, come on, what about letting me set you up with one guy, if it's a total disaster, I won't mention it again."

"Ugh. Fine. Deal."

Abrianna claps her hands with excitement, "Yes!"

~~~

My last set up ended up being with a gay guy, so you can understand my hesitation while I sit in The Terra Cotta Coffeehouse waiting for the guy named Devin who Abrianna assures me will be simultaneously gorgeous, sweet, and straight. I sip on my hot cup of mocha, watching the steam rise while the minutes pass.

He is already ten minutes late, maybe he saw me through the window and changed his mind. The door creaks and in walks a boy who looks like the pictures Abrianna has been obsessively sending me for the last two days. He is tall with jet black hair and a smile worth a million dollars.

I suddenly sit up straight and try desperately to look cool and unaffected.

"Hi, you must be Birdie. I'm Devin."

"Hi, Devin."

"Sorry I'm late."

"No problem. What's your major?" I ask as if I did not already know everything about him.

"English. I hope to be a teacher one day. You?"

"Psychology, but I'm not sure what I want to do with it yet."

Twenty minutes later and Devin and I are getting along. I feel some sparks, not like the ones with Austen, but something.

"Listen, I'm going to a party tomorrow night, you wanna come? You can bring some friends."

"Sure. I'll give you my number and you can text me."

"Awesome."

Devin must not find me completely repulsive so that is a good start.

~~~

Abrianna is on my arm as we walk in. I opted for my trust Nirvana t-shirt tonight, but Abrianna made it sexier by tying it in a knot at the end, now it's a crop top. Showing my stomach is nerve-racking, I can't believe I let her talk me into this. We make our way to the beer keg, feeling like we are old pros at drinking by now, even though we still have no idea what we're doing.

Devin finds me and hugs me, "Wow, you look hot! I'm so glad you came tonight."

"Devin?"

Devin and I turn around to see Mia and Austen.

"Mia? I didn't know you were coming here."

"Are you dating her?" Mia's southern drawl seems more pronounced than before.

"No, I mean, we just went on one date and I asked her here tonight. Are you dating this guy?" Devin asks while pointing at Austen, who looks just as confused as I am.

"No, I mean, kind of, but it's not serious."

"What the hell, Mia?"

"Sorry, Austen. I just thought we were being chill."

"Okay, I guess. Who's this guy?"

"Her ex." Devin seems to be standing taller as he says this.

Abrianna flashes me an 'oh crap' face and I do the same.

I look up to Devin who has completely forgotten I exist as he stares intently at the beautiful blonde on Austen's arm.

"I can't believe you're dating this guy."

"I don't need this, man. I'm going outside. You comin', Mia?"

Mia looks to Austen then back at Devin, "Sorry, Austen, but I need a minute with Devin."

"Whatever." Austen saunters off, clearly pissed.

Abrianna grabs my arm, "Let's go see what is going on somewhere else, Birdie," once outside, we find Austen.

"I'm sorry, Austen, I didn't know he is Mia's ex. He is just in a class of mine and I thought he would be cute for Birdie."

"Whatever, I don't care that much, I mean I like her but it's not like I'm in love with her or anything." Austen looks to me as he says this.

Abrianna leaves Austen and I to go talk to a friend of hers from class, or maybe she is trying to give us some alone time, I can't tell.

"Well, this night is way too dramatic for my liking."

"You want a beer?"

"Sure, I need to drink this night away."

~~~

Many beers later and Austen is officially drunk. I have never seen him quite like this, the closest was the night he knocked on my door and insisted on sleeping in bed, but I think he is worse tonight.

"Austen, do you want me to take you back to your dorm?"

"Why? Too drunk am I?" Austen laughs at this but I'm not sure why.

"Well, you can't stand up straight and I don't want you to get sick."

"Fine, fine, fine. You think Mia's hookin' up with that guy right now?" Oh geez, I hope so.

195

"It doesn't matter Austen, forget her."

"You'd like that wouldn't you?" More than you know.

"I just want you to be happy."

"Well, I'm not, haven't been since you. But you didn't love me back." Oh no, he's going to say something he will regret later, I have to end this now.

"Come on, I'll get you Chinese food if you come with me." Drunk people like food, right?

"Okay, geez." Austen has one arm over my shoulder as we inch our way out the party and down the street.

There's a great Chinese food restaurant in Alfred. It is open late into the night, capitalizing on the drunk college students searching for food.

Austen is sitting on the ground, leaning back on the building when I come out with his food. It's about one in the morning now and the streetlamp is illuminating him. With his arm resting on his bended knee, his eyes closed, his head back against the building, he might be the most handsome he's ever been. I'm not the only one who notices because a hoard of giggly girls are taking pictures of him.

"Stop, he doesn't want his picture taken right now."

"Are you his girlfriend?"

"No."

"He's so hot," says the blonde in front while her friends leans over and pukes. I hope Austen doesn't do that.

"Birdie?"

"Yeah, here's some food, Austen. I didn't know what you like so I just got some chicken fried rice, I think everyone likes that."

"Thans." I think he is trying to say thanks.

Austen holds the food in his hand but never opens his eyes or makes a move to eat it. I need to get him back to his room before he falls asleep here.

"Come on, we're almost there," I say as I tug on his arm, encouraging him to get up.

"Okay, I'm coming."

~~~

One eternity later and we are in Austen's dorm room. I get him onto his bed then try to say goodnight, but he's not having it.

"Don' leave, Bird."

"You want me to sleep here?"

"Please."

Austen falls asleep seconds later, I pull his blanket over him and take off his shoes. I consider staying here but I decide against it, I don't think sober Austen would want that.

The stars are peeking through the breaks in the clouds on my walk home, while love peeks through the cracks in my heart.

Chapter Thirty-Three

The sidewalks are wet from the melting snow as I stroll back to my dorm after having coffee with Abrianna.

I spot a package leaned up against my door with a note taped to the outside that reads: Elizabeth Wright, this is a donation from the college. Enjoy.

I open the package to find a brand-new computer. My first computer, ever. My jaw drops. How did the school even know I did not have a computer? Is it because I am in the library too much? This will make the next three years so much easier for me, I can now do my homework in my dorm room like everyone else on campus.

Tears are flowing freely now. This is one of the most generous things that I have ever experienced.

I race down the hall to Abrianna's room, pounding on the door, "Abrianna! I know we were just together but open up, I have to show you something.

Abrianna opens the door, "What's up? Why are you crying?"

"They're happy tears. The college has given me a computer," I say as I hold up the box to show her.

"What? Why? Did you ask for it?"

"No, I don't even know how they knew, other than the fact that I am at the library all of the time, I have never told anyone but you guys."

"Hmmm . . . I don't know, Birdie. I don't think this came from the school. I don't think schools do that."

"That's what the note said, who else could have done it?"

"Does David know you needed a computer?"

"No, I've never mentioned it to him."

"Do you think Austen did it, Birdie?"

"Austen? Why wouldn't he sign it then?"

"Maybe he doesn't want you to know."

"Should I ask him if he did this?"

"No, he didn't want you to know so don't say anything, but I think that is who did this. Colleges don't just give out computers randomly."

"Okay, I won't say anything."

Hope floats to the top, maybe he does still love me.

~~~

I don't ask Austen about the computer, but I do check with the administrator's office and they confirm that Abrianna was right.

"Sorry miss, I don't know who gave you that, but it was not the university."

"Thanks for clarifying, I think I have an idea who did."

~~~

It's Austen's birthday today and I want to give him a gift. It's a warm enough evening for me to have short sleeves on and, yes, I am wearing my trusty Nirvana t-shirt. I promise myself to get a more expansive wardrobe this summer, although I don't really mind the nickname Nirvana Girl. It's way better than Creeper.

I want to do some grand, romantic gesture like in the movies to win back Austen, but I have not the slightest clue how to. An idea came to me a couple of nights ago as I passed by the art studio where my painting is on display. I was too nervous to go in and see it hanging there, afraid it would look ridiculous next to the real artists. In the window looking into the bottom floor of the studio, I noticed some small figurines. I tapped on the window and the girl making them came outside.

"Yeah?"

"Did you make all of these?"

"Yes, I did."

"They are so cool."

"Thanks."

"You don't happen to have one of a turtle, do you?"

"A turtle? No, I have some similar animals, a couple frogs and a lizard. I can make a turtle pretty easily, though."

"Could you? If I paid you? I have fifty dollars from work I could give you if you could make me a turtle sometime tonight and have it ready for me tomorrow."

"It takes a little bit longer to make it. I would need until Monday night. I have to cook it in the kiln, it's a whole process. I'd be happy to if Monday is okay."

"I can make that happen. Can I get you the cash when I come to pick it up?"

"Sure, give me your number and I will text you when it is ready."

I just picked up the turtle and it is nine p.m. now, a bit late but that is okay. I have a piece of paper that I have written a quote on and plan to set it outside Austen's door with the note tucked underneath. I will knock and then quickly run away hoping he does not see me, and hoping he is actually in the dorm room to get the turtle instead of it falling into someone else's hands.

The note is a quote from, what else, *Pride and Prejudice*. It reads: *I cannot fix on the hour, or the spot, or the look or the words, which laid the foundation. It is too long ago. I was in the middle before I knew that I had begun. Happy Birthday.*

I did not sign the note, I will not have to because he will know it is from me. I walk up the steps to the second floor, to his room, I know it is his dorm room and I set the turtle on the floor, tuck the note underneath his belly and take a few deep breaths. I knock lightly.

"Coming." I recognize Austen's voice immediately and I race back down the stairs and don't stop running until I am back in my room.

Chapter Thirty-Four

I am not sure what I was expecting after the turtle gift, but this is not it. It has been twenty-four hours and I have not heard from Austen once. I pull up Austen's Instagram page for some hint or clue. My heart jumps when I see a new picture posted—one of the turtle that I got him, with a heart emoji as the caption. Maybe he is trying to tell me something. Does the heart mean he loves the turtle or me?

I lay the phone on my chest and look up at my dreamy purple string lights when my phone beeps.

It's Abrianna. Where are you right now?

I type back immediately: My dorm room. Y?

Come to the gallery ASAP.

Y?

Just get here. And hurry.

Why does Abrianna want me to go to the gallery? I know my painting is hanging there but so what? I scurry about, putting my shoes on before heading out the door. Spring in Alfred, New York, is lively and energetic with the buzzing of college students. The greenery of the trees and grass is mesmerizing, and the air is still cool in the evenings but the sun teases warmth in the afternoons.

I bolt to the gallery, clutching the necklace Austen got as I walk in.

I hear Abrianna before I see her, "Hey, psst."

"What's going on?"

Abrianna puts her finger to her lips, shushing me, then points to something behind me. I turn around and spot my painting and someone standing in front of it. It's Austen. Abrianna nods at me, urging me to go to him. I walk up slowly behind him, desperate to find the perfect words.

Austen hears my footsteps and turns towards me. He

looks startled.

"Hey, Birdie. I didn't know you'd be here."

"Hi, Austen. What's up? How are you?" My heart is beating so fast it hurts.

"I'm good . . . I stopped in to see this gallery, I was told it was pretty cool. I didn't know you had a painting here."

"Oh, well, it's nothing. My professor liked it and asked to hang it here."

Austen nods, "I'm glad you are here, actually, because I wanted thank you for the birthday gift."

"Oh, um, you're welcome. It was nothing."

"I'm sorry I haven't said anything about it sooner," Austen pauses, then turns back to the painting, "when did you paint this?"

"It was my final for art class last semester."

Austen walks up to it so he can examine it closely.

"It's of the night we spent here, right?"

The painting has small glowing yellow lights rising from blades of grass, the stars in the night sky twinkling above. A bottle of pink Moscato is laying on its side to the left of the frame, a turtle necklace is draped over the label, the bottle half empty. Next to the bottle lays a book, my favorite book, of course.

"It is. The idea was that I was supposed to paint something that represents happiness to me."

"Is that my turtle necklace?"

"Yes." Austen turns to look at me when I say this, intensely looking into my eyes.

"Is that your copy of *Pride and Prejudice* next to the wine?"

"Yes."

"You didn't have your book with you that night."

"I did, it was in my backpack. I wanted to include it in the painting because it makes me happy."

"Why'd you pick that night?"

"Um, well, that night was special to me. . . honestly, it was the best night of my life."

Austen looks back at the painting and rubs his hand on his chin, "That night was amazing for me, too, you know."

"It was?"

Austen is looking at me with big, nervous eyes. He chews on his bottom lip but does not say anything more.

My heart is beating so hard, I am worried it will leap from my chest, "I'm so sorry I screwed it up."

"I know. I know you didn't mean to, Birdie." I am blushing furiously now.

"Austen, did you give me that computer?"

Austen pauses, then says, "Yeah, I did, but I didn't want you to know it was from me."

"Why did you do it?"

"You have to have a computer, Birdie. I mean, it's the 21st century."

"Oh . . . thank you, Austen. It's made my life so much easier."

"You're welcome." Austen is clearly nervous; he fidgets nervously by rubbing his chin with his index finger. I think he wants to say something but is holding back. This is the moment to be brave. I don't want to be afraid anymore.

I hold my breath and say, "I know I didn't say it at the time, I was too afraid to, but I do love you. I love you so much it hurts and I'm sorry I didn't tell you that night or a million times afterward."

Austen's eyes go wide, his mouth drops open, "You do?"

"Yes, and I understand that you may not love me anymore, I hear you, I know you want to just be friends. If that is what you really want, tell me now, and I will never bring it up again, I promise. I will let you go if I have to."

"I still love you, Birdie."

"Really?"

"Never stopped," Austen grabs me by the waist and lifts me off the ground, kissing my lips as he does.

Epilogue

I am twenty-three now, and even though I graduated from Alfred University Magna Cum Laude, I am still struggling at my barely-above-minimum wage job to support my ridiculously tiny apartment in the heart of New York City. I love my job, and my apartment, though. I work as a court advocate for kids in the foster care system, using my past in the system to help the kids in it now.

On this cold Thursday night in February, I reminisce about those summer nights spent among the fireflies. I bundle a thick gray blanket around my shoulders and grip a cup of tea while I flip through, what else, *Pride and Prejudice*. New York City is outside my window; my purple twinkle lights are wrapped around the window frame, casting that purple aura I love so much.

I had better go to bed and try to get some sleep because tomorrow is Valentine's Day and it's going to be one heck of a day.

~~~

I'm late. I can't believe I am late to this. As the maid of honor, Abrianna will kill me if I don't hurry up.

My heels are clapping against the wet pavement. My long red dress is flowing behind me as I race inside the small building. Abrianna and Evan wanted a small ceremony with only twenty people inside the same, beautiful studio where Evan proposed—while a local artist painted their portrait. It was the most romantic thing I could ever imagine, and no one deserved it more than Abrianna. They reconciled sophomore year, Evan winning her back finally after spending weeks bringing her flowers every day. Apparently, he broke it off because his parents got in his head, threatening to cut him off if he didn't. They were worried she was distracting him from his schoolwork and football, but they have since come around and love Abrianna as much as the rest of us.

I push open the small, unassuming door and walk into a studio decorated with white and red roses. A few rows of white chairs and with rose petals scattered in between the rows, it turned out beautifully. Aiesha runs up to me as soon as I come in.

"She is in the back, Birdie, and she looks so beautiful."

"Of course, she does, I will go see her. You look great by the way," I run to the back bathroom and see Abrianna sitting on a bench in a long, flowery, beautiful off-white-colored gown. Her curls are pushed away from her face with a sparkly headband that I helped her pick out.

"Oh my god, Abrianna, you're stunning."

"Birdie! You're just in time, I think we're ready to start. I'm so nervous. You sure I look okay?"

"You look sensational." Abrianna smiles and I take a mental picture of her in this moment to keep forever. She has led such a marvelous life, graduating from Alfred to become a best-selling author. Her work is titled: *From Foster Care to Alfred.* Yup, she cowrote an autobiography with me about my life just as she promised. My favorite part of the book is the dedication that Abrianna insisted on writing: "I would like to dedicate this book to my best friend Birdie who is not only the subject matter of this story but the most inspiring person I have ever met." We both have made a nice chunk of change off my story, affording me a bunch of new clothes.

"The boys were out last night for a last-minute bachelor party type of thing. I think Austen and my dad are in rough shape. You had better keep an eye on him."

"Oh god, silly boys. Are you ready for me to stand at the altar?"

"Go ahead, I'll see you soon."

We embrace and I'm already crying. I pick up the end of my long red dress and walk the short distance up to the altar, smiling at a clearly struggling Austen who looks like he is about to pass out. However, even hungover, he is still gorgeous.

"You look amazing, Birdie."

"Thanks, love. I wish I could say the same about you. Long night?"

"You have no idea . . . I can't wait to tell you all about it later. Is she ready?"

"She is. Go ahead and turn on the music. Where's Evan?"

"I'll get him."

My father is kind enough to come all the way from New Hope to conduct the ceremony. He has become an important figure in my friend group's lives and was thrilled when Abrianna asked him to do it. He was able to keep being the priest at the church in New Hope even after he revealed that he had a child, me, out of wedlock because of how much he is loved by the community. He has a reputation now as being a sort of bad boy amongst the religious community which I find hilarious since he never does anything but volunteer at charities and pray.

"I hope that you will have a wedding of your own soon Birdie."

"I know dad and I will, but right now Austen and I are just enjoying life. I'm only twenty-three, there is no need to rush things."

"But you're living in sin,"

"DAD, please."

"Okay, fine. I just want the best for you, Birdie. I like

Austen but he needs to propose if he wants to stay on my good side."

"Today is about Abrianna and Evan, not me."

"Fine, fine." I love these arguments I have with my dad.

Evan and Austen make their way down the aisle, Evan looks a nervous wreck but also happy. Aiesha is in the front row along with Abrianna's parents and brothers. Evan's parents and grandmother are sitting on the other side along with a couple of aunts and uncles and their kids.

The music starts, everyone stands, and Abrianna descends the aisle, her beauty unmatched and her happiness radiating. This might not be a big group of people in my life, but they are undoubtedly the best people in the world. I spot Malcolm and his boyfriend Marcus in the back row looking as dashing as ever. Malcolm finally came out to his and Aiesha's parents last year and it has been tough, but he is happy to report that they handled it better than he expected.

Austen's mother is here with her new husband. She finally found out about all of Heath's cheating and left him. She is now happily remarried to her divorce lawyer who helped ensure that she walked away with most of the family's wealth. Turns out, Heath was not the money maker of the family, but Mary was. After she graduated from Alfred University, she went on to get an MBA from Harvard. She accumulated the vast majority of their income, leaving Heath with next to nothing when the divorce was settled.

Liza is no longer part of our friend group, I heard that she went on to marry some rich old guy. Aiesha kicked her out of her apartment shortly before my sophomore year at Alfred because she caught her sleeping with her boyfriend at the time. She has not spoken to her since.

Aiesha is enjoying singledom and is just as carefree and charismatic as ever while running her very own yoga studio.

I look at Abrianna, the twinkling lights I hung on the arbor yesterday intertwined between the roses is casting a beautiful glow over the bride, or maybe she is the one casting the glow. As she and Evan recite their vows, I peek over to Austen, his face lights up and he smiles at me with love in his eyes.

www.blossomspringpublishing.com

Made in the USA
Monee, IL
16 July 2021